Also by Laura J. Kendall:

The Kendall Rose Mystery Series

A Simple Case of Revenge

A Simple Case of Betrayal

A Simple Case of Payback

Novella

Hurricane Deadly

Find Laura J. Kendall's books on amazon.com

A Simple Case of Suicide!?

Laura J. Kendall

Dedication

For Mr. B my soul dog. I miss you more than words can say. Run free over the rainbow bridge until we meet again.

Acknowledgements

Thank you to all the amazing people who have supported me through the years of writing this book. It wasn't easy, but it was worth it!

Thank you to my editor Diana St. Lifer for editing my book in 2012. Your expertise has made this book look professional and complete. You rock!

Thank you to all the emergency service providers I have had the pleasure of working with for the past 30 years. Your dedication to serving others has been a beautiful source of power and inspiration.

A Simple Case of Suicide

One

Willow Run, New Jersey

Monday, April 1st

4 a.m.

The needle sliced cleanly through the skin searing its way toward a vein as he jammed his knee into her shoulder, crushing it into the mattress. Damn, she was a fighter. He pressed his knee harder, looking down at the trembling woman, so beautiful, staring back at him through blood shot eyes. He thought back to earlier when she'd welcomed his hard thrusts. Sadly there was no other way out. Not for a scheming bitch like her!

Beads of sweat glistened on his forehead, dripping down his face. He hesitated for a moment then drew back on the syringe, watching her dark blood flow into the chamber, mixing with the heroin floating inside it.

A muted groan came from the woman's duct-taped mouth as he let his eyes devour the scantily clad woman. Tears streamed down her beautiful face and just for moment guilt welled up in him. After all, he'd taken an oath to help not harm.

"Stop struggling bitch. You don't want to enter Heaven with a frown on that pretty face of yours, do you?"

He cupped her chin with his hand. "Do you?" Winking he shook his head sadly. "Trying to pin the pregnancy on me was your first mistake sweetheart," he said, wickedly, locking eyes with her, "But threatening to go public, well that was pure stupidity. Actually it is going to prove fatal." Smiling, he pushed the plunger hard shooting the liquid into her system. "Bye, bye Cheona."

Only minutes passed before the drug started to take effect. He felt her struggle die beneath him; her body sagged, relaxing against her will. Stepping back into the shadows surrounding the canopied bed, he timed her breathing with the second hand on his Rolex.

At three breaths a minute he had an overwhelming attack of conscious, nearly reaching for the bedside phone to call for paramedics. He willed himself to turn away. It had to be done. Her breaths now came two a minute. He ran his fingers through his hair as he paced the room.

Like a guppy she inhaled one last, slow breath.

Carefully he removed the duct tape from her mouth and lowered his lips to hers. Parting them with his tongue he inhaled deeply sucking her remaining breath into his body.

Two

She jerked up in bed, smacking the blaring alarm clock with her hand. It fell to the floor with a thud.

"Darn it's just not human to get up this early," she grumbled to the yellow lab lying beside her.

Lightly, her hand stroked the soft fur. "Sure wish I was rich. I'd have the maid bring me breakfast in bed."

"Huff!" The dog slapped a big paw against her leg.

"OK yours, too."

She swung her legs off the bed onto the carpeted floor. "Time to rise and shine sleepy head," she said to the dog.

Stumbling through the dark room she hit the light switch on the wall, illuminating the cozy room. This apartment was no comparison to the opulent lifestyle she lived when her parents were alive. But sadly that was a lifetime ago.

Walking into the kitchen, she readied the animals' breakfasts, which the dog and cat greedily gulped down. "You two act like you haven't been fed in a week," she said, laughing.

By six she'd showered, made up her face, and dried her waist-length blonde hair.

"Bela, come!" she called.

Bela, the love of her life for the past five years and a mutt of quiet distinction, looked like a yellow lab on the outside. But beneath that gentle exterior, lay the heart of a Rottweiler.

They'd met at the Bloomingdale animal shelter where she'd told the attendant she wanted to adopt a small dog. Smiling, the worker guided her past the other dogs to the last cage on the left.

"Here's the closest thing we've got," she said with merry eyes.

"I sense a problem," said Kendall.

Kneeling, she came nose to snout with a yellow dog, weighing close to one hundred pounds. Liquid brown eyes looked expectantly into hers.

"She's really a good dog."

"But?" said Kendall, looking up at the standing worker.

"Let's just say she came in with the name Loco Bela."

"Loco Bela, huh?" Slipping her hand through the chain link gate she stroked the gentle giant's soft head. "So you're a crazy white dog?"

"Woof!" The deep bark filled the air as the yellow dog playfully licked her hand. "You're the first person she's taken a liking to. Usually she chases them off one way or the other," said the girl.

"I guess she was just waiting for the right person to own. And Bela-girl, I think you've just found her."

"Woof!"

Five years later they were still happily together with a bond that made them family. With her tail wagging and leash in mouth, the lab mix trotted over to Kendall.

Several minutes later and happily refreshed by the morning walk, she slid behind the wheel of her 1979 Firebird. The muscle car's engine roared to life with the twist of the key.

Three

She hated fighting rush-hour traffic on route 80 east, bound for Wayne General Hospital. Commuting in a small car and squished between tractor-trailers and buses going seventy miles an hour made her tense.

Forty-five minutes later she relaxed as she waved at a passing William Paterson University police car and made a right into the driveway of the Wayne General Paramedics.

Sure she needed the overtime, but something smelled funny about this shift. She thought back to the pleading phone call from her boss yesterday. He practically begged her to come in so he wouldn't have to shut down a medic truck, and then was suspiciously evasive when she asked with whom she'd be working.

Pulling into headquarters at 6:45, she got her answer in the form of a blue Dodge Viper, sporting vanity plates with the letters CJ. She put the Firebird in park, not wanting to get out.

Geez, why couldn't the boss man have just warned her? At least she could've prepared herself mentally for twelve hours of unrelenting tension. She shut the engine and slowly got out of the car. Think positive. Maybe today would be a good thing, bringing healing to them both.

She grabbed her stuff from the back seat and walked toward headquarters, a three-bedroom, white house, with the nickname 'The White House." Only this sure wasn't a place where George Washington had slept. Looking up, she saw a short brunette glaring at her through the front window.

Healing huh? Yeah and pigs can fly.

CJ Wagner whipped open the door. "What are you doing here?" she snapped.

Kendall brushed past her not looking the angry woman in the eyes, "Good morning to you, too, CJ."

With a thud she slapped her knapsack on the table and turned around. "To answer your question I'm covering a sick out."

CJ slammed the door. "Oh that's just wonderful!"

"My sentiments exactly," quipped Kendall. She pulled her utility belt from the knapsack, wrapped it around her waist, and clipped the front. From the charger she took a portable radio and dropped it in the holster. "Believe me if I'd known..."

CJ held up her hand. "You would have never said you would cover." She clasped her hands in front. "It's not your fault. I was just caught by surprise, that's all." She walked out to the garage that housed the two medic trucks, ALS 12 and ALS 13.

Kendall followed. Silently they started the shift vehicle check. By seven, the suburban, bearing the call name of Advanced Life Support Thirteen, or ALS 13 for short, was stocked and ready for any emergency thrown their way.

Once they'd been good partners and great friends. Kendall shook her head silently reliving the incident that had broken the trust between them. She wished it had never happened. But it had, and nothing could erase it.

Kendall glanced at CJ busily counting the narcotics and momentarily softened. "Feel like getting something to eat?"

CJ looked up and smiled weakly . "Sure, just let me wash up."

For five years they had been partners on the ten-to-ten shift. Their morning routine had been to check the truck, breeze over to the King George Diner for a hearty breakfast, and pray for a silent radio.

"The diner all right?" asked Kendall.

"Sounds good to me," said CJ as she shut the faucet. Opening the passenger door she climbed in. "Come on let's go."

A few minutes later, with jingling keys slapping against their thighs, they walked to a booth and sat down.

The waitress came over smiling from ear to ear. "You two back together?"

Kendall nodded. "We're back together all right, at least for today Julie."

"Hey everybody, look who's here," Julie yelled.

Blank stares and raised eyebrows answered back.

"Well it has been almost a year." Julie shrugged her shoulders and took out her pad. "The usual?"

"If you can remember that I'll nominate you for waitress of the year," CJ said, her grin spreading across her heart-shaped face.

"You," she pointed to Kendall, "will have two eggs well, no hash browns, and wheat toast."

Kendall nodded.

"And you will have three eggs over easy, bacon, home fries and hold the..." she stopped mid-sentence.

The tones for ALS 13 reverberated through the diner. Small talk stopped as patrons listened to the male dispatcher, "ALS 13, respond in to Willow Run—10 Melody Lane for an unconscious female."

"13 received and responding," answered Kendall on her portable.

"Oh well, thanks anyway Julie," said CJ. She patted the woman's arm. "You still get my vote."

"Mine, too," called Kendall going out the door.

Plopping the key in the ignition she started the medic truck, pulling down the visor mirror, she quickly applied a fresh coat of light pink lip gloss then brushed her feathered blonde hair. Turning to CJ she said, "Ready?"

CJ nodded and smiled.. "You'll look great for the unresponsive patient." She opened her bag and took out her chap stick. "Nice gloss."

"Thanks," said Kendall, as she turned the truck onto Hamburg Turnpike with lights flashing.

CJ gingerly applied the lip balm as Kendall hit the siren, leaving the diner behind.

Four

Barreling down Hamburg Turnpike she made a right onto Valley Road speeding through Wayne, Oakland, and into Willow Run.

At the bottom of a steep long hill, rightly named Breakneck Road, Kendall turned onto Harmony Lane and briskly passed an ornate sign welcoming them to Willow Run— a gated community that prides itself on family safety and privacy.

ALS 13 headed up a sloping hill to the guard shack that sat between two massive stone pillars. Getting into Willow Run is no easy matter for the average citizen. Today, however, the pair's uniforms assured them hassle-free entry. Pulling along the side of an open window in the stone guard shack, Kendall nodded to the guard Sam, a retired Wayne cop.

"Security will lead you in," he said. He pointed to a white Ford Taurus with a flashing yellow light bar. "Hate to sound cliché, but follow that car!"

The Taurus peeled out, kicking up a storm of loose gravel as it sprinted away.

"Think he'll get the hint we aren't exactly driving a sports car?" asked CJ

"Do they ever?" quipped Kendall.

"How in God's name do people make enough money to buy something that big?" exclaimed CJ. She pointed to a winding driveway leading up to an enormous home overlooking Lazy Creek.

Kendall glanced at her partner. "I can't believe you just said that!"

"What?" said CJ?

"Come on now Ms. Money Pants."

CJ shook her head. "Nope not even with all my dad's money." CJ laughed. "Guess I know who is buying breakfast later."

"Yeah, if we ever get to eat, and let me tell you my stomach is starting to growl."

CJ nodded in agreement. "Amazing how far those three families have come isn't it?"

Twenty years prior, three wealthy families—the Blacks, the Harrisons, and the Rowens—had purchased six hundred acres and gated it off from the neighboring towns of Franklin Lakes, Oakland, and Wayne. Forming an alliance, they had sold parcels of land, no less than ten acres and several up to one hundred acres. They kept, of course, three of the best estates for themselves. The families had amassed fortunes.

Up ahead, the Taurus slowed down.

"Looks like rent-a-cop finally took the hint," CJ said.

Melody Lane ran circuitously around the entire gated community with estates lining its route. The Taurus squealed to a stop and ALS13 passed it coming around a bend. She hit the brakes hard, slowing to thirty miles per hour.

The road was jammed with police, fire, and EMS vehicles.

"Must be somebody real important," said Kendall.

"Who isn't in this town?" quipped CJ.

They parked behind a New Jersey state trooper car and got out.

Five

A handsome blonde, dressed from head to toe in a dark navy uniform, met them at the bottom of the driveway. His pants sported a yellow stripe running the full length of his well-defined legs. On his left shoulder, a white patch with blue and yellow thread proclaimed him an officer of the Willow Run Police Department.

"Hello ladies, I'm Officer Black." He reached out and took the monitor from Kendall's hand. "Here, let me carry that. Looks like a suicide. We really appreciate you doing the pronouncement."

"It's a D.O.A.?" asked Kendall.

"Yes, she was the live-in-maid." He turned waiting for them to follow, his silver badge dull in the dreary light. "We've only done a quick investigation, but from the looks of it she shot up some heroin and overdosed. From the note we found I'd say she wasn't a very happy girl."

"OK." CJ put the medication bag and airway kit back in the truck. "Lead the way."

The three of them walked between a line of police officers, volunteer ambulance EMTs, and firefighters standing outside the front door.

"Why so many people for a suicide?" asked Kendall.

Ignoring her question, Black picked up the pace then slowed, allowing the medics to pass through the front door ahead of him. "Keep going straight through the entrance hall and into the kitchen," he said as he pointed the way.

Ah, good looking but deaf, Kendall thought as she studied his handsome features. Shrugging her shoulders she continued walking onto expensive tile, her eyes traveling the length of the entranceway.

The home, easily 6,000 square feet, opened into a wide entrance foyer with staircases on both sides ascending to the second floor. Suspended in the middle of the ceiling, an enormous crystal chandelier cast bright light over the green-blue tile floor.

Passing below the second-floor balcony, they walked down a hall, entering a family great room that opened into a gourmet kitchen on the right.

At a large, white oak table sat a man and woman in their mid-forties and a male teenager. Behind them a crackling fire blazed in the hearth. Off the kitchen to the right was a door leading to the maid's quarters.

Kendall stepped through it into a hallway, simply decorated with pale pink flower wallpaper. Berber carpet ran the full length, ending at another door.

"Some place," said CJ. "Kind of makes my house look small."

Kendall stopped in front of the closed door. "This it?"

"Yes, go right in." He nodded his head back toward the kitchen. "The son is the one who found her."

Kendall glanced back casually. "What time was that?"

Black flipped open his notepad. "According to the son, he came home around 6:30 a.m. and ..."

"Did you say came home?" interrupted Kendall. "He looks a little young to be out so late."

"Yes that is correct." He glanced at the pad. "The boy said he wanted a shirt for the morning. When he couldn't find it, he went to ask the maid where it was."

"I wouldn't want her job," said CJ.

"Gee, and there just happens to be an opening, too. Leave an application on your way out," Kendall said, pushing open the door with a twist of the knob.

Black shoved by, crushing her against the wall. "She's in the bedroom," He trotted through an open door disappearing with the monitor.

Kendall peeled herself off the wall. "Good looking, deaf, and a little high strung," she muttered.

Surveying the room as she did every scene, she slowly walked into the bedroom behind CJ. She never knew what little detail picked up on initial glance would come back to play an important clue later.

Officer Black glanced at his watch. "We got here at 6:45. It is now 7:30 and I'd say by the looks of it, she killed herself about five minutes before the boy got home."

Kendall raised her eyebrows skeptically. "What makes you say five minutes Officer Black?"

"Well..." he loosened his tie. His Adam's apple moved gracefully with a deep swallow. "I guess I said that because when I first got here she still felt warm."

Kendall met his emerald green eyes with blue ones. "Anything else we should know?"

"No, that about covers it." His lips crinkled into a nervous smile.

"Why wasn't CPR started if she was still warm, Officer Black?" she said softly.

He stiffened momentarily. "Well, um."

CJ rolled her eyes and nudged Kendall. "Typical cop answer. Come on partner, let's get this over with." Pulling out a trip sheet she motioned a red-faced Officer Black to the side and started asking questions.

Kendall picked up the monitor Black had set down by the door and walked over to the white-laced canopied bed. Before touching the patient, she quickly glanced around the bed and immediate surrounding area. To the right of the bed was a small table with a large Tiffany lamp. The bright multi-colored light cast a sparkling rainbow over a spoon, lighter, and latex tourniquet. An empty bottle of vodka lay tipped over on its side.

Where the hell is the needle? Maybe she snorted instead of shooting up, thought Kendall. She shook her head, glancing back at a latex tourniquet strung casually on the bed.

Carefully, she pulled the thick, white comforter off the victim's face, exposing a strikingly beautiful and deeply tanned female who looked no more than twenty years old. Pressing her fingers into the woman's neck, she felt no pulsation in the carotid artery. What a waste of life.

Hadn't Black said something about it being a suicide? Again she searched the area for an uncapped needle, and then began an in-depth exam, mentally noting each finding.

The icy cold of death seeped through her gloves as she touched the victim's hand almost causing her to recoil. The girl's perfectly manicured nail beds glowed deep purple. She pulled a small flashlight from her pocket and shined it into the female's vacant, brown eyes. "Pupils pinpoint and fixed without reaction."

"What's your guess on downtime Kendall?"

She jumped up, startled by a deep and all too familiar masculine voice.

Six

Straightening, she turned to face her six-foot buff ex-boyfriend, New Jersey State Trooper Mike Garcia.

"Hello Mike," she said, willing her voice to remain calm. "Sorry, I can't even give you a hint yet. I just started the exam."

She turned back to the patient silently wondering just what the hell he was doing here.

He didn't move. Clearing his voice he said softly, "So how are you?"

"I really don't think this is an appropriate time for small talk Mike."

"The state police are taking over this investigation." He let out a sigh.. "So you'll be reporting to me."

She didn't bother turning around as she muttered, "Whatever you say Mike."

"Can you give me a rough estimate?" He cleared his throat. "It's important."

"First answer a question I have." She faced him. "Is this being considered a suicide?"

"Where did you hear that?"

"Does it matter?"

"Yes." He looked down at her putting his hand under her chin to lift her face to meet his. "Who?"

She shrugged her shoulders. Mike was the most bull-headed man she knew. That's what made him so good at his job, but bad at relationships. His job certainly made him good at interrogation, a skill he'd practiced frequently on her.

Angrily she backed away letting his hand fall from her face and drop to his side. "What difference does it make Mike? I overheard it, OK?"

His stare penetrated her. "Still little miss loyalty, huh?"

Straightening her back, she dismissed him with a flash of her startling blue eyes.

"Sorry."

She didn't answer. After everything he'd put her through, he didn't deserve to be in the same air space much less giving her a hard time. She turned back to the patient.

Lifting the monitor onto the bed, Kendall set it down next to the girl's legs. Removing the leads from a side pouch, she attached four electrodes, one to each wire. The black wire she placed on the girl's left upper chest, white on the right side, red on the left lower leg, and green on the right leg.

Flipping on the monitor she waited for the gray screen to tell her the patient's heart rhythm.

"What does the monitor say?"

"You still here Mike?" She shook her head. "Don't you have someone else to boss around or interrogate?"

"I said I was sorry."

She pushed the record button and gently held the paper as it printed out into her hand. "Go away Mike. I promise you'll be the first..." She glanced over at CJ still talking to Officer Black. "Actually you'll be the second one to know." She nodded in CJ's direction and Mike's eyes followed her lead.

She should have taken great pleasure in seeing his strong face turn stark white as sweat beads suddenly broke out on his forehead. She should have, but she didn't. "You remember my old partner CJ, right Mike?"

He couldn't meet her eyes. "Let me know what you find," he said stammering as he backed out of the room.

Continuing the exam, Kendall smiled sadly. If he hadn't hurt her so badly, she'd feel a kindred spirit in him. Like him she was good at her job, bad at finding lasting love, and good at taking care of strangers. She pulled the comforter down, fully exposing the dead woman's body.

Since Mike won't answer her question, she'd start with a blank slate. Methodically, she checked the corpse. The girl was dressed in a short, lacy camisole with matching panties. Her arms were straight at her side. Her legs pressed tightly together. Starting again at the head, she felt the skin, checking temperature, color, and texture. Pupils were fixed and constricted, non-reactive to light, which is consistent with a narcotic overdose. Rolling the woman on her side she noted the buttocks and backside of both arms and legs were a dark purple color where blood had pooled—a natural condition of death called dependent lividity. On the right arm, there was a single track mark. The blood long since clotted. Carefully she searched the area again for a used needle. Nothing else struck fear into the heart of a paramedic more than an addict's uncapped needle. Getting stuck with one sentenced you to at least a year of terror getting tested for HIV, Hepatitis, and a host of other diseases.

Slowly she lifted the girl's arm. It was then she spotted a fine red line circling the wrist. Leaning over, she checked the other arm, finding one there too.

Moving down the bed to each leg she noted circumferential red marks on both ankles. The left ankle also had a faint tint of blood where something had invaded the skin tissues.

Geez, had the poor girl been bound before she died? Kendall felt the area, estimating whatever had caused the wound to be about 1.5 inches thick. She'd make sure to check with the medical examiner to see if the woman had sex before she shot up.

Maybe it was simple kinky sex or maybe someone caused the woman's death accidentally. She shook her head feeling in her gut this was most likely on purpose.

Inch by inch she combed the corpse looking for track marks. There wasn't another, not even between the toes or on the stomach.

Staring ahead she frowned. In the fifteen years she'd been a medic, she couldn't remember one call where a person had intentionally killed herself with heroin. Accidental OD sure. Hundreds of cases she'd seen and saved using the narcotic blocking drug Narcan. But a first-time user knowing enough about drugs to kill herself? She didn't buy it for a minute. No way!

Seven

Something wasn't right!

She pulled the leads off the body and tucked them back into the monitor's case. She'd find Mike and tell him what she thought. Remembering what Officer Black had casually mentioned regarding the down time, she swiveled around to look for him and nearly knocked his well-built body to the floor.

"What are you doing?" she asked. "How long have you been standing there?"

"I was just watching your exam." He held up his hand. "Sorry I didn't mean to startle you." The corners of his mouth turned up in a warm smile revealing straight, white teeth.

He stood around five ten, with a clean-shaven boyish face and golden-blonde, crew cut hair. He looked so handsome and so darn young.

Returning his smile, she said, "No I'm sorry for jumping all over you." She pulled the comforter up over the body then lifted the monitor off the bed. "I guess I'm feeling a little stressed."

His sheepish gaze traveled her body from head to toe, finally settling back on her face. "We all are. Having someone so young commit suicide should upset everyone. If you start to lose feelings for the people you come in contact with, it's time to get out of the field."

She quizzically raised her eyebrows. "How do you know she killed herself?"

He cocked his head. "A note was found beside the body. Didn't Trooper Garcia tell you?"

"No. In fact when I asked him about, it he demanded to know who had told me it was a suicide." She patted his arm lightly. "Don't worry I never give up my sources."

His strained face relaxed into any easy grin. "I had no idea it was a secret. Looks like I owe you one agent 99." He winked conspiratorially and began to hum the theme to Get Smart.

"Oh Max you do go on so." She inched by him. "I'll just go tell the chief what I've found. Maybe then he'll let me under the cone of silence and declassify the information." Peeling off her latex gloves, she held out her hand. "Good to meet you Officer Black."

He matched her strong grip. "Call me Johnnie."

She glanced down at the entwined pair. "Nice cuff-link."

Releasing his grip he fingered the metal. "Thanks. It's my family crest. Unfortunately," he said holding out his other arm, "I lost one somewhere."

"I'll keep an eye out for it," she said, looking at him directly. "So back to my first question Officer Black. Why wasn't CPR started initially?"

His emerald green eyes didn't waver from her. "Honestly, we saw all the drug paraphernalia and figured she was gone." His jaw tightened. "Did we do something wrong?"

Patting his arm lightly, she shook her head. "No not this time. She was gone long before you got here. I was just curious because you had said she felt warm."

He looked down at his freshly polished boots.

She rubbed her forehead. "Look, I'm sorry if I've upset you. I assure you no amount of CPR was going to bring this one back." She cleared her throat.

He raised his head.

"You did nothing wrong Officer."

His demeanor brightened. "Thanks for saying that. I really respect the paramedics. I'd hate it if you thought I was some goof-ball cop."

"Well, ya know, if the shoe fits..." She smiled and then punched him soundly in the arm. "Again, it was very nice meeting you." She pointed out the door. "I've got to give an update to Trooper Garcia."

Black scowled. "What are the staties doing here anyway?"

She shrugged. "That is a mystery, isn't it?"

Eight

Mike was in the kitchen talking with the family. Nodding to her as she entered the room, he said, "I'll be with you in a minute Paramedic Rose." He turned back to the Garrison family, now numbering four.

His eyes followed Kendall as she walked through the kitchen and out to the foyer.

"So you came home what time again Billy?"

Billy Garrison, all of seventeen years, wrung his hands together. "Ah... around 6:30 I guess." He looked wildly around the room then back at his parents. "Why? Am I in trouble?"

Mike jotted down some notes leaving Billy's question hanging in the air for a minute. "Not yet son. I'm just covering all the bases." Turning his steely gaze on the fourth member of the family who had arrived moments earlier, he continued questioning.

Looking the thin male up and down he noted the fire-department gear he was wearing. "You're the fire chief of Willow Run correct?"

Jack Garrison coughed. "Yes. I've been out at a fire alarm since 2:30 this morning." He brushed dirt off his blue work pants. "We just finished with clean up a short time ago. I came home as soon as I heard." His voice faltered, cracking with undisguised emotion.

"Then we shouldn't have any problem verifying your whereabouts should we?" Mike stated.

Jack swallowed deeply. "Well, the call may have wrapped up earlier. I'd have to check with the desk for official times."

"That's OK; I'll take care of it." Mike leaned down, placing his arms on the table in front of Jack.

To his right Mark Garrison jumped up, pounding his fist on the solid table. "Trooper!"

"Sit down, Dr. Garrison."

"Trooper Garcia I suggest you stop harassing my family and finish up this investigation quickly!" He straightened his tie. "I have a very busy day at the hospital."

Mike raised his impressive frame, towering above the doctor. "That is precisely what I am doing sir."

Lowering his face inches from Mark Garrison's, he said softly, "What I'd like your son to explain is why we found this in the drawer of Cheona Carpenter's nightstand." He tossed a handwritten note on the table.

Mark Garrison picked it up and began reading it. Mike watched the doctor's face blanche a sickly white color. Garrison shook the paper in front of Jack. "Explain this son."

Jack kept his eyes averted.

"Were you involved with the maid?" snapped the doctor. "For God's sake...you screwed a common maid?"

Jack stammered. "We were in love dad."

Garrison looked incredulous. "In love? Please don't insult my intelligence. She was just a pretty piece of ass. Why the hell do you think I hired her in the first place?"

Janice Garrison gasped. "I won't have that talk in my home!" Picking up her white hanky, she dabbed her eyes. "Our son would never be involved with the help. Would you Jackie?"

"I loved her mommy," Jack whispered.

Mark Garrison tapped the letter. "From what I've read, it seems she didn't share your feelings."

"She was just confused." Jack broke into tears laying his head on the table. "I loved her and now she's gone. Don't any of you have a heart? Why would she do it? Why? I wanted to marry her."

"Marry her? Never!" shouted Mark Garrison. "I didn't raise you to dabble with some trollop." He raised his fist. "If I had known, I would have ended it. No questions asked."

Jack stood up, turning his back to his father and looking to Mike. "May I go now sir?"

Mike nodded. "Don't leave New Jersey. I'll have further questions for you."

Jack stormed out of the room throwing his family a look of disdain.

Mark Garrison glared at the trooper." We are not saying anything more until we have our lawyer present."

"Have something to hide doctor?" Mike closed his notebook. "Very well Dr. Garrison, you may call your lawyer. For now you are free to go as is your son Jack."

Nine

He sauntered over to the foyer looking for Kendall and found her in the library gazing at the books stacked from floor to ceiling in built-in mahogany bookcases. "Colonel Mustard, in the library, with the candle stick," he whispered.

Startled, Kendall jumped. "Geez Mike, you scared the heck out of me."

Holding the palm of her hand over her rapidly beating heart, she shook her head. "However, after careful deduction, I believe it was Mrs. Peacock, in the maid's quarters, with a needle full of heroin."

"Come on outside with me," he said.

Together they walked over the perfect lawn and down to the street where they stopped beside his unmarked trooper car parked at the curb.

She stood next to him, but not close.

Leaning back against the dark car he said, "So what have you got for me Ms. Rose?"

"I have a few questions for starters." She waited for him to get angry. When he did nothing more than shuffle his well-polished combat boots, she looked up.

"Go ahead shoot," he said, jovially.

"Don't tempt me Mike." She felt herself slipping back into the easy way it had been between them. Maybe a little too easy, she mused.

His blue eyes twinkled back at her. Quickly regaining her professional facade she shot him the question. "Is this being classified a suicide or not?"

"Tell me your findings first," he countered. "Along with your gut feelings."

Anger glinted in her eyes. "Why do you have to be such a pain in the ass?"

"Just hear me out Kendall." He held up his hand. "OK?" Exhaling loudly, he continued. "I want your opinion first. I don't want what I tell you to influence anything." He tapped the side of the cruiser with his hand.

She leaned back where his hand had been. "OK, you win." She paused a moment to collect her thoughts. "I can't tell you anything conclusive. That's for the Medical Examiner to do." She looked across the plush, green lawn. "But I'll give you my findings and...," she patted her stomach, "my gut."

"That's all I ask." He reached out touching her shoulder lightly. "Despite what happened between us, there is nobody I trust more than you to give me a straight answer."

She did not meet his gaze. "First the girl wasn't an IV drug user..."

"We found a needle containing heroin still in her vein," he interrupted.

"That may be all well and good Mike."

They locked eyes. He moved to face her.

"Intimidation isn't going to work." She placed her hand on his broad chest. "So back off, or I'm out of here."

"Not another word." He held up his hand. "Swear.""Did you check her body for track marks?"

"She had a friggin' needle sticking out of her arm. What more do we need than that?"

"Yeah, well if you had bothered to look you'd have only found that one. No old ones. No recent puncture marks healing. I even checked between her toes and she has nothing!" She made a face. "Doesn't it seem odd to you that a first time user killed herself?"

"She overdosed." He kicked a pebble across the blacktop. "Come on, Kendall. In our jobs we see drug OD's all the time."

"Ever see one use heroin to commit suicide?"

He shrugged his broad shoulders.

"Fine!" She held up her hand. "What about the circumferential marks around both wrists and ankles?"

"Marks?"

"Yeah, they look like rope burns, Mike, and they are there if you'd just do your job and look!" She cleared her throat. "Did she have sex before she died?"

"I don't know yet."

"The son found her around 6:30 right?"

He nodded.

"By the time I examined her, it was a little past 7:30. When I walked in, one of the Willow Run cops said he figured she been dead only five minutes before the kid found her." She shook her head. "The girl already had rigor in her jaw which takes over three hours to set in."

He leaned forward. "Go on."

"She was cold as ice. No way had she died a little before 6:30."

"So she's been dead at least three, maybe four hours." He checked his watch. "That makes her overdosing around four am."

"The M.E. will be able to really fix time of death, but that is my estimate."

"That's what I was figuring. She shot herself up way before 6:30." He rubbed his forehead. "Makes you wonder why a good-looking girl like that would want to kill herself. You never know the problems people have. Things look good from the outside, but inside things are a big ol' mess."

"What the heck are you talking about? This is not a simple overdose!" she snapped. Holding up her hands, she continued. "Not with those red marks and no sign she's a user." Dropping her hand to her side, she said firmly, "I'd suspect foul play if I were you Mike."

He ran his fingers through his short, layered, brown hair. "Look Kendall, we found a suicide note next to her. Makes it pretty clear to me she overdosed on purpose. Stop trying to read into things like you always do!" He fingered his weapon.

Kendall stomped her feet. "Read into things, huh? Well let me state for the record, Mr. State Trooper, that I think something's not right with this scene and you need to look into it more."

He looked down into her eyes, searching for an ounce of understanding for the position he'd been put in. When her eyes held none, he said, "I'm the law here not you, and as far as I am concerned this case is closed."

"Mike, please stop being so pig-headed and..."

He held up his hand. "I'm not in the mood to fight with you Kendall."

Kendall grimaced. "Oh, you're not in the mood?" She tapped his chest with her pointer finger. "Mark my word Garcia, this isn't a simple case of suicide! There is something far more sinister at work here starting with the way you are conducting this investigation, and I'm going to prove it."

His eyes flashed with anger. "Stay out of it Kendall. The state police are in charge of this investigation, not the paramedics!" He shook his finger at her. "You take care of the sickly and injured, and I'll take care of the police work darlin."

Ten

Silence hung heavily in the air between them.

"Still as stuck on yourself as ever I see," she said angrily, turning away. "Since you won't listen to reason, I guess I have nothing more to say."

"Wait," he said, reaching for her arm. "Can I see you again?"

"What's the point? I think she was murdered and you don't. I guess you win Mike, just like you always do."

"I need to talk to you." He nodded to a passing officer. Lowering his voice he leaned into her. "Alone."

"Why? So you can tell me how stupid I am or maybe you want to ease your guilty conscience? Save it!" She walked away without looking back.

He wasn't going to hurt her again. Just being so close to him brought back memories sweet, intimate, and in the end, heartbreaking.

She put the monitor in the truck and slipped behind the wheel. Her body sagged with exhaustion. Flipping on CBS 101.1, the local oldies music station, she closed her eyes and waited for CJ to finish her end of the pronouncement.

A tap on the window jolted her, sending her heart racing for the second time on this God-forsaken call.

Officer Black stood outside the medic unit. He motioned for her to lower the window.

She hit the button. "Hi. What's up?"

"I was wondering where you disappeared to." He rested his hands on the windowsill. "Is everything all right?"

"Trooper Garcia had a few questions for me." She checked her pager for the time. "I'd better go find my partner."

Slowly opening the door she stepped out heading for the house. Black walked easily beside her making small talk. As they reached the front door CJ met them.

"I'm set," she said.

"Me too," said Kendall.

CJ brushed by them.

"Something I said?" Black pointed at CJ's retreating form.

Kendall shook her head. "If I even began to tell you the sordid dynamics going on here you won't believe it."

"Try me," he said.

She laughed sarcastically. "You don't have enough time." She tapped his watch. "And we've been out of service here long enough."

She turned to leave and he stepped closer. "Um."

"What?" she asked.

"I was wondering if you might like to go out some time?"

She met his gaze. "I think I'm a little too old for you Officer Black."

Nervously he cleared his throat. "Call me Johnnie. Let me be frank with you Kendall. I'm twenty seven and you don't look a day over thirty so what's the problem?"

"Johnnie, you are one of the most handsome, far sighted men I've ever met." She patted his arm and laughed. "I am very flattered, but I'd be robbing the cradle."

"Tell me the age difference." He held his hand to his chest. "Which, by the way, will mean nothing to me"

"How does thirteen years hit ya?"

"Numbers don't matter. What matters is how you feel inside. Plus the outside is looking pretty good to me."

She shook her head. "Johnnie you're very sweet. You made my day."

"When are you off next?"

"You can't be serious?"

He pulled a notepad from his uniform front pocket and began to write. Ripping off the sheet he handed it to her. "Here are the numbers to my cell phone, pager, and home. I'm very serious."

She took the paper gently in her hand.

He handed her a blank sheet and his pen. "And yours?"

She hesitated, shuffling her feet on the gravel.

He extended his open palm. "Come on...fair is fair."

Giving in to his charm, she scribbled down her cell phone number and handed him back the paper.

"What time will you be home?"

"My shift ends at seven, and barring any late calls I should be home by eight."

"Great, I'll call you tonight."

Eleven

She waved good-bye to Officer Black and walked to ALS 13 where CJ was waiting in the passenger's seat.

"Did that cute cop just ask you out?"

"Yeah, can you believe it?"

"Of course I can. You're a beautiful woman. Any guy would be lucky to have you," CJ said squeezing Kendall's hand. "I mean it."

"Thanks CJ." She flipped down the mirror applying gloss with a quick sweep.

"I'd give anything to undo what I did. I miss our friendship so much."

"Me too." She gripped the wheel. "But let's not talk anymore today. Between riding with you and seeing Mike, I can't take much more." Closing the mirror, she leaned back in her seat, rubbing her neck with her hand.

CJ whitened . "Did he see you?"

"Yes, and he's heading the investigation."

"Talk about an awkward scene. I am so sorry Kendall."

"I know you are." She turned the key. "Let's just drop it for now."

CJ leaned against the window. "Since when is the state police in charge of a local death investigation?"

"Good question, and one I forgot to ask him."

"He actually had the nerve to talk to you?" She tapped her long nails on the radio console. "Unbelievable!"

"More like grill me than have a conversation." Kendall waved at the guard as they drove out of Willow Run. "So what did you make of the call?"

CJ exhaled loudly. "Something smells rotten in Denmark."

"Those are my feelings exactly." Kendall picked up the radio mike. "ALS 13 to dispatch. We are back available on a pronouncement."

"Received ALS 13 at 8:35," answered a male dispatcher.

CJ turned up the disco song playing. "I checked her myself, after you told me what you found on the physical exam." She gritted her teeth. "There wasn't another track mark on her."

"Oh you didn't hear?"

"Hear what?" asked CJ.

"Mike has finished his investigation and has determined this is a simple case of suicide."

"What?!" CJ lowered the radio. "You've got to be kidding me. Nobody intentionally kills herself that way and she sure as heck was not a drug user."

"My thoughts exactly." Kendall turned into the lot arriving back at the diner. "How would she know what to do?" Spotting a space she gunned ALS 13 narrowly beating another car. "Unless she had some help."

Shutting off the truck, she said smartly, "Who knows? Maybe suicide by intravenous injection is the new rage."

"I don't think so," said CJ.

"Me neither." Clearing her throat, Kendall continued, "But we're only paramedics, not cops, so there is nothing we can do."

"Isn't there?" CJ squeezed Kendall's arm. "I say we prove mister macho man wrong."

"If you have an idea spit it out because I'd like nothing more," Kendall said, clipping the keys onto her belt.

"We have friends in higher places than law enforcement." CJ smiled and opened her door.

Kendall followed. Patting CJ's back she said, "You're right girlfriend. I really should give you credit for more than your good looks."

CJ flipped her shoulder length brown hair and walked inside.

By 10:30, their stomachs were full and a plan was being made.

Twelve

They say everyone has an epiphany at some point in their life and Mike Garcia's had come at the tender age of five. He believed they would ever be free from him, until one sweltering night a neighbor had finally taken pity.

A wave of blue burst through the door and pulled his drunken father off his mother. Then a gleaming, golden triangle found his bruised body hiding under the table. A trooper dressed in an immaculate, French blue uniform knelt on his hands and knees, bringing him eye level with little Mike.

In a deep, calm voice, the officer said, "It's over son. Come on out. He can't hurt you anymore." He held out his hand. "My name's Trooper Dave."

Mike placed his small hand in the biggest one he'd ever seen. "Want to drive my cruiser?"

Mike got his first lesson that night. Not just a lesson in driving, but also a lesson in life. That night he swore to himself that one day he would be a New Jersey State Trooper, and no other little kids or their moms would ever be hurt again.

Eighteen years later, he reached his goal and graduated from the State Police Academy in Sea girt, N.J., after completing twenty-two weeks of intensive, around-the-clock training.

He remembered the night drill instructor Dave Hampton burst into the bunkroom at three in the morning, screaming at the top of his drill sergeant lungs. With a smirk and barely concealed smile, Hampton ordered the recruits to run at full speed down to the beach wearing only their skivvies to collect individual grains of sand and fill their freshly polished shoes with the scratchy gravel.

After filling them he screamed at them to "dump out the damn sand and get back to the barrack recruits!" Mike was up until six a.m. polishing the shoes, he scuffed with sand.

This was one of the many tests designed to break a recruit's spirits, to weed out the weak who didn't deserve to be a New Jersey State Trooper.

Mike had taken every one of their tests and passed with flying colors, believing if you want something badly enough you'll do anything to get it.

The day he walked up to the platform to receive his badge had been one of the proudest moments in his life. In the audience, sitting in the first row, was his mom, pride radiating from her loving face.

And waiting on stage, in honor of their special relationship, stood Trooper Hampton. Trooper Dave walked up to the mike, telling everyone about the day, eighteen years ago, when he'd taken the hand of a small, frightened boy and gone for the ride of his life in a troop car.

When the laughter finally died down, Dave proudly handed Mike his badge, officially welcoming him to the New Jersey State Police.

How do you thank a man who'd become your mentor and whom you loved like a father? Shaking his hand, Mike pulled him into a bear hug, thanking him for a life he never dreamed he could have.

Fifteen years later Mike still loved his job. He was proud to wear the uniform of the state police.

He gazed up at the massive chandelier suspended above him and silently went over the facts of this case.

Even this job has its downfalls and today was one of them. The case was not going as smoothly as he would like.

There's always a fine line of power when troopers worked with local police. He hated stepping on toes and since his arrival, he felt like he'd been walking a tightrope.

A summons from the governor is not something one takes lightly. The governor insisted the state police handle this case. Mike couldn't be sure why. Lower level troopers like himself were on a need-to-know basis and apparently he didn't need to know.

Historically, Willow Run has always been a hard town to control no matter who was governing. Heck, money equaled power, and the leaders of Willow Run sure had no problem using theirs to get what they wanted. But not this time. Not with Mike stuck right in the middle of this mess.

The Willow Run cops weren't happy to see Mike, and he didn't blame them.

Seeing Kendall only added to the tension. His heart nearly stopped when he walked into the room and saw her. She as strong-minded and beautiful as ever and just as unforgiving. If only he could go back and undo the damage he'd done. She was the one woman who had touched his heart since his divorce and he blew it big time. He destroyed the one prize he now would give anything for, and that was her undying love for him.

"Uh Trooper Garcia?"

Mike looked into the eyes of a rookie state trooper he'd been training when he received this assignment. He brought her along for some scene investigation experience.

"Yes Trooper Connell, what is it?"

"Uh, I was just wondering when we were going to be able to get some breakfast. I really need to eat something soon or..."

"Or what?" he said sharply. "Look at me when I speak to you Connell."

Her mud-brown eyes popped up meeting his. "Yes sir."

He pointed at his cruiser. "Go sit in the car and wait for me."

"But sir," she stammered.

Mike held up his hand. "Trooper Connell, let me lay this out for you. I'm in the middle of conducting an investigation." He jabbed his finger at her. "I don't have time to take a crap much less take you to breakfast."

He turned to go, then stopped and looked back at the stunned woman. "One word of advice that may sound sexist, but frankly I don't care. In this field, a woman has to be twice as good as a man to get any recognition. Doesn't sound fair or pretty, but like it or not that's the way it is. Whining about being hungry isn't going to earn you any brownie points. Now go wait in the car. I'll be out as soon as I can."

Shoulders slumped, the rookie shuffled down the driveway.

"Oh and Trooper Connell."

Like a puppy dog awaiting a scrap she halted. Turning around she said brightly, "Yes, sir?"

"Put on your hat Trooper."

Quickly she plopped her French blue hat onto her head, its triangle of gold glinting in the stormy sky. "Sir yes sir," she said, her face red with shame.

Walking up the white, brick steps, he glanced at the silver medical examiner's van idling in the driveway.

He liked the new medical examiner, Bob Crosby. His scene investigators were always thorough and professional. With luck, there were just a few loose ends to tie up and he'd be out of here and out from under the steely glare of the Willow Run PD.

Thirteen

It had all been so easy. Sure he felt bad, even guilty at first. But he had done the right thing. She was becoming too much of a liability. If she opened those sweet lips of hers like she had her legs, she would have ruined his career. He had worked far too hard to get where he was today, and he'd be damned if he would allow her to take everything away from him.

The investigation seemed to be going as planned, except for the medics sticking their noses where they didn't belong. He chuckled to himself. You know what they say about curiosity and the cat. If they caused him any trouble he'd deal with them just like he dealt with Cheona.

Rubbing both hands together, he watched the body being loaded into the van for the trip to the medical examiner's office. Of course nothing would be found to incriminate him. Not with his connections. The doors to the van slammed soundly and he smiled with the anticipation of the case being closed. "Bye-bye darling," he whispered.

She'd been dynamite in bed. Shy at first, but what a willing student. He grew hard thinking about all the raunchy things she'd done to him and for him. By the end, she had become his well-trained whore. The van drove down the street and with it his problems. Ah, life was good. At least it will be once Cheona is buried beneath a beautifully carved tombstone.

He let the curtain fall back over the window knowing it was time to get back to the investigation. He left the room as quietly as he had come.

Fourteen

Kendall and CJ sat at headquarters going over the notes they made during breakfast. It was now three p.m. and the day remained quiet with not a single call since the pronouncement.

"So the guy who owns the house is a doctor?" asked CJ.

"Yup and he's a well known trauma surgeon from Saint Joseph's Hospital." Kendall brushed the end of her nose with her pointer finger. "Which does explain the huge mansion he lives in darling, but not the dead maid in his basement."

"Maybe they had an affair and he dumped her?" CJ tapped the table with her pen.

"So she offed herself with heroin?" Kendall took a sip of mint herbal tea. "After doing this job for fifteen years nothing would surprise me."

"I'll nose around the hospital and see what I can find out," said CJ.

"Oh those nurses do love to talk." Kendall laughed. "I'll chat with the medical examiner. The autopsy should be finished by tomorrow, but the toxicology reports will take a while."

CJ was staring at her. "What?" said Kendall.

"Nothing, it is just good to have you back," CJ said.. "I know you don't want to talk about what happened, but someday we need to clear the air. OK?"

"Deal," Kendall said as she extended her hand.

"Deal," CJ agreed, and they shook hands.

"Now let's brainstorm some..."

The tones went off. "ALS 13 respond in Paterson. The Christopher Columbus Housing Projects, building number one, tenth floor stairwell for an overdose."

"Geez! Are we surrounded by heroin today or what?" CJ spat.

"Now come on girlfriend it could be cocaine."

CJ rolled her eyes, grabbing her stethoscope as she got up from the couch and followed Kendall out to the garage.

Kendall slipped behind the wheel of ALS 13 and started the vehicle.

"Either way, I'm sick of dealing with addicts!" CJ dialed up Paterson Fire Department's radio channel. "ALS 13 to fire; we are responding CCP."

Paterson fire dispatch answered confirming the address.

Kendall hit the high-low siren at the light, making a left onto Hamburg Turnpike. Traffic was thick. Some drivers yielded to the right, while others played a popular game called "let's out run the medic truck."

A small red compact swerved into their lane cutting them off to make a left turn.

"Hope it's your mother jackass!" Kendall yelled at the driver. She slammed the brakes hard, skidding to the right. "Where's a cop when you need one?"

Behind them another siren blared. CJ glanced in her mirror and smiled. "You were saying Kendall."

A blue and white, Wayne police car shot past them following the red car. The officer gave them thumbs up as he sped past.

"OK, I take that back."

Fifteen

Twelve minutes later they turned into the parking lot of CCP. Behind them a Paterson Fire Department ambulance pulled in and parked. Kendall groaned, not wanting to get out into a day that had turned cool and cloudy. A brisk wind stirred up the trash littering the sidewalk and flinging it against the truck.

Sighing with resignation, Kendall hopped out into the howling wind, begging the rain to hold off until the end of shift. "Damn!" she exclaimed as a wet piece of dirty paper hit her face. "I hate this place."

"I second that," said CJ, grabbing equipment from the back of ALS 13.

Meeting up with the stretcher-wheeling EMTs, they headed down the narrow steps leading to the burnt-out entrance. A broken, metal door swung on its loose hinges, hitting the cement with a bang. CCP was the most dangerous area in the city of Paterson, full of drugs, shootings, and gang wars. It was made up of four high-rise building with two single-story buildings sitting between them. It is a great place for the high-class yuppies to buy their smack, if they don't get killed trying.

In New Jersey, the emergency medical system is a tiered response. Utilizing the local or state police to respond and render initial care, followed by volunteer or paid emergency medical technicians who provide basic first aid care and oxygen.

Paramedics in New Jersey are paid professionals, working in teams of two for the local hospitals. Medics are supposed to be called out only to the scenes of serious medical or traumatic emergencies. Then working in conjunction with the other basic level responders, they provide advanced care to the patients.

When the system worked well, it was great. When it didn't, it was a nightmare.

Kendall scanned the area for the local police, angry at their absence. What she found working in Paterson is the police rarely showed up at the projects, far too busy with regular police work. Unfortunately that left EMS alone to fend for themselves, and it riled her to no end.

The Wayne General Paramedics and two Paterson Fire Department EMTs, warily made their way down the stairway making them easy marks without police protection. From time to time each one of them would glance up, checking for an open window.

Last year the dope dealers had been dropping water or sand-filled liter soda bottles onto unsuspecting emergency responders. Until the game had gone horribly wrong with the gangsters missing their intended target, hitting a resident in the head and paralyzing him from the neck down.

Kendall hated coming here. Why not just stick a big, multi-colored, bull's eye on her back. Face it ,they were outnumbered, sitting, little ducks without a police presence. This crap hole was the only place in the city where she truly was afraid.

Up ahead she saw a large group of black males. One of them—a short kid with a red, gang bandana around his head—was dealing out dope like it was candy.

Something about him caught Kendall's eye; something familiar she couldn't place. Boldly she watched his scarred hands give a bag of white stuff to an even younger boy in return for cash. Except for the bandana, he wasn't badly dressed. Maybe it was the stark white dress shirt that stood out from the filth or the tons of shiny gold jewelry flashing from his fingers and neck.

She quickly averted her eyes when he caught her staring. Her team was no match for seasoned dealers and addicts, and she wanted no confrontation. Where are the damn cops? she thought angrily.

"Hey sweet thing. You like what you see?" He smacked his lips together and winked. Holding out his hand he said, "Maybe you'd like some of my fine candy?"

Kendall let her smile cover her fear. "Thanks, but no thanks. Sounds like we have one of your customers down on the tenth floor. Now you wouldn't want us to miss saving you a future deal, would ya?"

"Hell no, blonde girl!" He motioned the other men away from the door-less entrance. "Back off yo. Let em do their job." He jerked his head at group of five hoods. "Hands off da ambulance people."

Kendall nodded at the dealer, easing between the gang members. They cautiously entered the building walking past the abandoned, vandalized security booth, which had been taken over by rats and cockroaches.

To the left were two elevators. One elevator was for the even floors and one for the odd. The doors to the even cab swung open, letting out a group of women and one child.

"Where you all goin'?" asked one woman dressed in a drab pair of jeans and crusty white tee-shirt.

"Tenth floor stairway ladies," said Paterson EMT Eddie Rodriquez.

"Oh," the woman said her speech slurring. "Lucky you got dis elevator then."

Eddie smiled. "That's right. I sure don't feel like lugging all this stuff up a flight of stairs."

She smiled back. "Well, honey, you look like youz in fine shape." The group of women left laughing. The kid stared wide-eyed at the group in uniform.

Kendall winked. "Hey Eddie, I think you could have gotten a date. She likes you, honey."

"Well you know what they say about us hot-blooded Latinos," He shoved the stretcher inside and patted the mattress. "You can find out any time you want."

CJ pushed them both into the pungent-smelling elevator. Eddie's rotund partner, a new guy named Rob, followed CJ in. "I do believe I smell urine," he said.

"Duh, that could be because you're standing in a puddle of it." Shaking his head, Eddie glanced down then back at Rob. "Hey bone head, nice job with the jump bag."

Rob grunted. Bending down, he yanked the blue canvas medical bag out of the yellow puddle swinging it toward the stretcher.

"Rookies!" said Kendall. She put out her gloved hand stopping the bag mid-swing. "Don't you dare put that pissed-soaked bag on the stretcher."

CJ hit the tenth-floor button. "Next stop, ladies lingerie."

"You tease," said Eddie.

The ancient elevator rattled and shook its way to the destination. Creaking open the rusty door revealed the tenth floor. Eddie held his hands up, checking the dimly lit hallway. "Looks clear ladies."

The rescuers cautiously left the safety of the elevator.

According to the hospital's "sitting duck policy," emergency personnel are not allowed to carry anything to protect themselves. Being the ever-compliant employees, Kendall fingered the mace hidden in her utility pouch while CJ flipped on her heavy-duty, black mag-lite. Kendall figured they were shoo-ins for employees of the month.

The group crept toward the metal door leading to the garbage strewn stairs. Eddie pushed it open slowly, filling the blackness with illuminating light. At the bottom of several steps was a landing where a still form lay amidst rodent droppings, urine puddles, and trash.

"Oh hippie-hippie, joy-joy," snarled CJ.

"You mean we have to go down there by ourselves?" asked Rob.

"Do you see anybody else volunteering?" asked Kendall. She followed Eddie down the steps. "OK everybody, watch out for needles."

Rob shuddered, blocking the doorway with his obese body. "No way," he muttered.

"Get going," CJ said.

He moved aside to let her by. "You go ahead."

CJ frowned. "What are you, chicken? Get down there and do your job."

"You first." He backed away from the top of the stairs.

CJ sneered and walked down to the landing. "Eddie your lame partner won't be joining us." She pointed up.

"Get your ass down here now or I'll call for a supervisor," shouted Eddie, busy ventilating the drug overdose with a bag-valve mask. "We need a blood pressure taken."

"I'm not touching that maggot," spat Rob.

Kendall ran through a bag of normal saline solution and started an intravenous line in the addict's left arm. "Let the coward be, Eddie. We don't need him."

She drew up two milligrams of the narcotic-blocking drug Narcan. "CJ, can you get the blood pressure and apply the monitor for me while I save this fine citizen's life?"

CJ shot Rob a disgusted look. "Sure no problem."

Minutes later the Narcan flooded the addict's system. Eddie dropped the bag-valve mask as the man took a deep breath on his own. Picking up his portable radio, Eddie called for a supervisor.

The addict began to moan, then sat up with a start. "What the hell you doin' ta me?"

Kendall turned to CJ. "Ah, once again we are miracle workers. Now this fine citizen can resume his productive place in society."

CJ pressed her hands together. "I'm so proud."

The addict pushed himself onto all fours. "Fuckin' wrecked my high bitch."

"Hey take it easy man, you overdosed," said Eddie.

"Yeah, you weren't breathing when we got here so chill out," said CJ

"You give me that Narcan shit?"

"Yup," said Kendall.

"I ain't goin' to no hospital." The addict stood up and swayed from side to side.

"Easy buddy," Eddie said, steadying the man with his hand.

The addict batted him away. "Get off me Spic." He stumbled down the hall leaving a trail of blood.

Kendall reeled in the bloody intravenous line, wrapped it around the saline bag, and threw it on the garbage-strewn cement.

She locked eyes with Rob at the top of the stairwell. "That guy's almost as big a loser as your partner Eddie." She spat on the wall. "Almost."

The fire department supervisor pulled behind the ambulance just as the responders were walking up the steps to the parking lot.

Kendall radioed dispatch. "ALS 13 available. Patient refused further treatment by walking away."

Dispatch crackled back amused. "Ah, the miracle of Narcan. Received ALS 13."

Rob was immediately relieved of his duty and Eddie was sent back to headquarters for another partner.

Kendall said, "Another day, another half-dollar."

CJ laughed. "You got it," She checked her watch. "The good news is we have only three more hours to go."

Sixteen

The dispatch radio crackled to life. "ALS 13 come in."

"13," answered CJ.

"Take it into Wayne, Breakneck Road for a serious motor vehicle accident with entrapment."

"ALS 13 received and responding."

Kendall flipped on the emergency lights and hit the gas shooting onto Matlock Street. "This is going to be a bit of a hike," she said.

"Sure is," CJ said and dialed Wayne police. "ALS 13 to Wayne PD. We are responding to Breakneck Road, coming out of Paterson."

"Wayne headquarters received."

The siren cut a path for the unit as it traveled quickly through Paterson, Haledon, and into Wayne at the top of Central Ave. They were passing Wayne General Hospital when the Nextel phone signaled an incoming call with two beeps.

"Hello," said a deep male voice over the hands-free speaker.

CJ and Kendall looked at each other.

"Is that who I think it is?" said CJ.

"It's him all right, and I'm sick of him so you answer it," Kendall hit the siren. "I've had my fill of him today."

CJ pushed the direct connection button. "What can we do for you Mike?"

"Put Kendall on."

"What no pleasantries Mike, like a simple hello?" said CJ angrily.

"Sorry CJ. Hello. Look I'm under some pressure here and I need to speak to Kendall...now!"

"You want to talk to him?" asked CJ.

Kendall yanked the wheel to the left, narrowly missing a car that had cut into the path of ALS 13. "I'm a little busy right now. Tell him we're on a call and I'll get back to him later."

CJ relayed the message curtly.

"Where is the call?" asked Mike.
CJ let out an exasperated sigh. "He just doesn't give up."

Kendall grabbed the phone and hit the off button. "Whoops!" she said sarcastically.

CJ smiled. "You go girl."

Breakneck Road hadn't been given its name for nothing. Up ahead at the top of the steep hill, a host of fire apparatus, police vehicles, and ambulances lined the road.

"Looks like a bad one," said CJ.

Kendall slowly drove past the emergency vehicles. A Wayne cop signaled them to continue down the hill. She stopped ALS 13 next to him and rolled down her window. "What have you got?" she said.

"Head on with two seriously injured. We have the bird on standby."

"Thanks," said Kendall.

Continuing down the hill lined with more emergency vehicles, they rounded a small curve and surveyed the scene for the first time. "Shit," said Kendall.

CJ let out a whoosh of air.

Kendall parked ALS 13 behind a volunteer ambulance from Willow Run. They got out, grabbed the equipment, and decided to split up rather than request another ALS unit for help.

Kendall took the first car, a small compact so badly damaged she couldn't tell the make or model. It had crossed the double yellow line and smashed head on into a new Ford Excursion SUV.

Setting down the trauma bag and monitor Kendall asked an EMT, "How many patients do we have?"

"Only the drivers of both vehicles." He pointed to the compact. "This one's unconscious."

Kendall squeezed past firefighters setting up the Jaws of Life and spotted a Wayne EMT holding c-spine stabilization in the car. "Hey Daria, what do you have?"

"The patient's unconscious and entrapped in the vehicle by both lower legs. No way to access the lower abdomen or chest due to the steering wheel and dash."

Kendall poked her head through the shattered driver's side window and felt the neck for a carotid pulse. "She's still got a strong carotid. Her breathing isn't cutting it. I'm going to have to intubate her."

CJ came over to her. "My patient's been extricated. I'm going to load and go to Saint Joe's. You take the chopper."

Kendall nodded. "OK thanks CJ. Leave ALS 13 and I'll have a cop or firefighter drive it and meet you at the ER."

"Sounds good girlfriend." She turned to leave, and then stopped. Tapping Kendall's shoulder she said, "Don't look now, but guess who showed up?"

Kendall glanced past CJ and saw Trooper Mike Garcia standing next to a Wayne cop. "This patient is in bad shape. I don't have time for him. Tell him that for me when you pass his interfering ass." She touched CJ's royal blue turnout coat. "Thanks partner."

CJ winked. "Happy to oblige."

Next to her, the jaws growled to life filling the air with the deafening sound of its engine. Kendall shouted across the car to the fire chief, startled to see it was one of the men Mike had questioned earlier at the Garrison home. Composing herself she said. "How long do you think it will be until you get her out?"

He shook his head. "She's pretty well entrapped. It's going to be a while."

Kendall nodded. "OK, then let me get my gear on. I have to get inside to tube her."

"No problem," He motioned his firefighters to get in place. "Anything you need, ask."

She pulled on a heavy, royal blue turn-out coat with "Paramedic" in bold, silver letters across the back, matching helmet, and gloves. Into the pockets she slipped all she would need to start a large, bore trauma intravenous line and airway equipment for putting a tube down into the patient's lungs.

Because of the high-speed impact, all the doors to the compact had been crushed shut. With the help of Chief Garrison, Kendall angled her body feet first through the passenger window. He lowered her slowly into the vehicle. "Do you have a name yet?" asked Kendall.

"The officer said the tag comes back to a Jill Newman."

Kendall tucked her body into the mangled seat next to the driver. The dash and steering wheel were pushed forward by the compact's displaced engine. Wrapped inside them sat an elderly female driver.

"Jill, can you hear me?" asked Kendall.

The patient moaned softly, but did not reply.

"Jill, I have to put a tube into your lungs to help you breath. It will feel real uncomfortable, but you need to cooperate and help me. OK?"

She quickly readied the equipment she needed to intubate the patient. The woman's respiratory rate was slowing down. Turning to Daria, who was holding spine stabilization from the back seat, she said, "I hate to nasally intubate someone with a head injury, but I don't have a choice." She applied K-Y jelly to the ET tube and bent the plastic tube into a circle to help the tube conform naturally to the patient's trachea.

"I'm ready to tube her, so keep a good grip. I don't want to move her spine."

"Ready," said Daria.

Kendall released the tube from the circle and slowly threaded it into the patient's right nasal passage. The trick was to listen for the patient to take a breath, and then pass the tube through the open vocal cords and into the lungs. On the patient's next breath she gently pushed the tube down into the patient's airway. A weak rush of air through the tube signaled it was in place.

"It's in," said Kendall. She reached for a long piece of fabric called twill tape and tied it around the tube and behind the patient's head. "Tube is secure. Daria, do you think you can bag her while I start the intravenous line?"

"Just let me rest my hands for one minute."

Kendall picked up the bag valve mask and turned on the oxygen tank. She carefully placed the bag valve's opening onto the end of the tracheal tube sticking out of the patient's nose.

"No problem. I'll bag and hold c-spine while you take a break." Using one hand to stabilize the patient's head she squeezed the bag valve mask sending much-needed oxygen into the patient's lungs.

Outside, the jaws crunched metal away from its path, fighting to free the severely injured patient from the tangled wreck of metal.

It is said that hearing is the last sense to go, so no matter what the patients' condition, Kendall always talked to them. One thing she always believed is that no one should ever die alone. "Hold on Jill, we'll get you out of here soon."

The car shook suddenly and shouts went up from the firefighters. The jaws engine went silent. "What was that?" asked Daria warily.

Garrison peeled back the safety blanket covering Kendall, Daria, and the patient. Leaning in through the shattered window he said, "A fire has broken out in the engine compartment. We are attempting to put it out now. If we can't knock it down, I'm pulling you both out!"

Kendall felt cool droplets of water. She reached out and gave Daria a quick squeeze on her hand. "We'll be OK. Are you up to bagging now?"

Daria nodded her head. She reached her arms over the back seat and molded them to the patient's, taking over the bag valve mask with her hands.

Kendall flipped on her mag-lite. The mass of metal blocked most of the patient's body except her shoulders to her head.. Searching the twisted dash and steel for the patient's hand or arm, Kendall found an opening wide enough to let her work.

"I smell smoke. Do you?" asked Daria calmly.

Kendall sniffed the air receiving a nose full of acidic smoke. Coughing, she peeled the safety blanket back and stuck her head out of the window. "We've got some smoke in the passenger compartment!" she shouted to the chief.

"The fire is out." He pulled back the blanket further. "We'll give you some fresh air. You girls OK?"

Kendall glanced back at Daria who raised her eyebrows, then smiled. "We'll make it," said Kendall.

Chief Garrison looked in at the patient. "How's she doing?"

Kendall spoke softly. "Not good. We need to get her out now."

Garrison hurried away from the car to the command truck, as the jaws growled back to life, gnashing and brutalizing its way to the victim.

Time was a precious commodity for this patient and it was running out fast. Reaching through the metallic hole Kendall snaked a sixteen-gauge needle into the woman's hand vein then connected a liter bag of normal saline. "Hang in there Jill!" she shouted over the jaws.

Pulling the safety blanket back over the three of them she settled in to wait. "Come on you guys," she whispered.

Seventeen

From the steps of the Oakland fire command center, he watched the drama unfolding before him. Shit, there had to be cops from every surrounding town helping out at the scene. One paramedic had left ten minutes ago with the first patient. The other one was still inside the damn car. Part of him wanted to go in there and pull her to safety. Part of him wanted the car to explode and end her interference. He'd see how far they'd take it. Hopefully the girls would lose interest and move on to something or someone else. So for now he'd bide his time watching their every move until he was sure they couldn't find anything to implicate him.

With a swat of his hand he directed a nosy photographer to move back behind the police car. Damn reporters always trying to capture someone's tragedy on film. Front-page news! If the guy took one more shot of him he'd rip the camera out of his hands and take care of the film. Hell, why stop at the film when he could rip away something far more precious, like the reporter's job.

A shout from a Wayne cop drew his attention. From up the hill a red Corvette sped down the road, barreling between the cones and flares, hell bent on going through the accident scene. Racing up the hill to help, he got to the car just as the Wayne cop threw the Vette into park and pulled open the driver's door.

Together they reached in and yanked the twenty-something-year-old male out. It wasn't much of a struggle and the asshole had his hands cuffed behind his back in a matter of seconds. If only the extrication could go this easily. He glanced back at the crash site when the jaws stopped.

The Wayne firefighters were on top of the car manually pulling the roof backwards with brute strength. Inside the car, the medic and the EMT looked upward as metal peeled away exposing the passenger compartment. It didn't take a brain surgeon to see the patient was pale as hell.

The medic pulled herself from the wreck, holding the IV above the entrapped patient. He could see the elderly woman was crashing fast. The firefighters wrapped a chain around the wheel and dash using the jaws' power, and yanked them off the patient freeing her from the metal tomb.

Eighteen

CJ followed her patient into the trauma room holding the intravenous line as the EMTs moved the cot next to the stretcher. On three, the two men lifted the patient strapped to a backboard onto the trauma gurney.

The trauma team gathered around the bed. "What's the story CJ?" asked Dr. Mark Garrison, head of the trauma team.

CJ glanced up, startled to see the renowned trauma surgeon at work so soon after what happened. "Two cars head on. The other driver was still entrapped when I left. This patient is a thirty-six-year-old male, belted driver of a Ford Excursion. The air bag deployed and he did not lose consciousness. The only injuries I find are lacerations to the forehead and right forearm. He also is complaining of slight chest pain, on palpation, which is directly in line with the seatbelt. Other than that everything else checks out fine. I'd say Mr. Hollenbeck is one lucky guy."

Dr. Garrison nodded. "Thank you." He waved his hand in the air. "OK everyone get busy."

The group broke up each going about their own specialty. The man was in good hands. CJ hoped the other patient would be as lucky.

She felt a tap on her shoulder. "Excuse me Paramedic Wagner."

She looked into the face of Mark Garrison. For such an imposing man he was small in stature, equal to CJ in her height of five foot four.

Impeccably dressed in a dark suit and bright white lab coat, he leaned forward conspiratorially. "May I speak with you a moment?" He stepped back and rubbed his hand over his red goatee.

"Sure Dr. Garrison," she said, pulling the monitor leads off the patient. "The second patient should be here any second with the helicopter, so I guess we have a few minutes."

He held open the trauma room door. "After you."

CJ walked through the door and into a hallway filled with EMT's and police officers.

"Busy day?" she said.

"Yes it is. Shall we go somewhere more private?"

CJ hesitated, suddenly aware this was not to be a conversation about the patient she had just dropped off. "Ah...sure." She walked toward the automatic doors leading outside to the ambulance bays. "Just let me grab my equipment out of the Wayne ambulance."

He followed her out. "You were one of the paramedics at my home this morning, were you not?"

"Yes, sir, I was." Grabbing the wall handle she hoisted herself into the back of the rig. She wound the leads around her hand then tucked them into the cardiac monitor's side pouch. Glancing back she saw the doctor climbing into the rig behind her. "Why don't we sit down?" He patted the bench seat beside him.

CJ stood up, feeling uncomfortable with the situation. "Dr. Garrison this isn't my rig. The crew will be coming back any minute," she stammered.

"Did you find anything unusual at my home this morning?"

"Cutting right to the chase huh? Doctor you know that I would be breaking patient confidentiality if I spoke with you about this."

"Yes, I realize that. But I am on the board of this hospital and indirectly your boss." He ran his hand over his baldhead. "So you can tell me."

"Dr. Garrison I can't believe you are putting me in such an uncomfortable position." She picked up the trauma bag and monitor. "If you need information, you can call my boss Mr. Carbone, and he can help you."

Beside them, a back-up alarm to an arriving ambulance sounded. From the window behind Garrison, CJ saw the Franklin Lakes ambulance backing in. She moved to pass him and he stuck out his leg.

"Paramedic Wagner may I please have your attention. I don't have much time."

She looked down at the skinny man. "Dr. Garrison, I'm sorry but I can't divulge patient information." She shook her head. "Not even to you."

He flashed her angry look. "All I want to know is if my maid kill herself like the press is saying?"

Press? What the hell was he talking about? Garrison was worried about something for sure, but what? Maybe she could use his determination to her own advantage. "What did the press say?"

"That she killed herself using heroin."

How the hell did the press get a hold of that? The investigation couldn't possibly be finished yet. Maybe good old Mike has a leak somewhere, she thought.

"Look Dr. Garrison, I can appreciate your position. I can't tell you anything, but I know the trooper heading the investigation." She pulled out her note pad and wrote down Mike's work number. Handing the paper to Garrison she said, "Here is his number. Call him and maybe he can answer your questions."

Garrison jumped when Kendall stuck her head in. "We've been in CPR for about twenty minutes. She's still in PEA on the monitor."

The three of them raced beside the stretcher being wheeled into Trauma Two.

"She's already intubated and has fifteen hundred of normal saline on board. She just lost her pulse as we were wheeling her to the chopper and they don't fly cardiac arrests, so we came by ground."

"Did she get Epinephrine?"

Kendall pushed a needle into the intravenous port. "Yes this is her fifth."

"Atropine?" he asked.

"She is at the maximum of three milligrams. She took a hard hit. Not much I could do at the scene."

Garrison softened. "Looks like you did all you could. Not much more we can do either, but we'll try."

They wheeled the cot next to the open trauma bed. "OK team, we have the second patient who is in cardiac arrest. She is in pulseless electrical activity; what should we do next?"

The team of residents eagerly listened to the surgeon. "No takers, huh? What is PEA?"

A resident held up his hand. "Pulseless electrical activity."

"Which means what?" asked Dr. Garrison.

"It means the electrical system of the heart is working so we get a good EKG rhythm, but the heart is not pumping," said the resident.

"So due to some catastrophic event, this one being a major accident, the patient has no pulse but the electrical system still functions so there is a beautiful cardiac rhythm on the monitor." Garrison waved his hand around, dramatically. "So what is it important to remember in the case of PEA?"

"To always check for a pulse and to treat the patient not the cardiac monitor," said a female resident.

"Very good Kerry. Since the paramedic has done the majority of treatment before getting here, what are some other things we can do before we call it?"

Kendall and CJ left the room and the buzz and chatter as the team called out suggestions. "Too bad about your patient," said CJ.

Kendall walked out head down. "No matter how long I do this job, I still can't get used to losing a patient I've worked my heart out to save. Poor lady was on her way home from visiting her daughter."

"How did you find that out?" asked CJ.

"The daughter showed up at the scene." She shook her head. "She watched her mother die." Climbing into the Franklin Lakes rig, she opened a cabinet and pulled out the antiseptic spray. Blood was everywhere. "This one really hit home for me because it dredged up a lot of memories of my mom and dad."

CJ hopped in and put her arm around Kendall's shoulders. "I don't know how you've handled all you've been thrown in life. I wish I hadn't added to the hurts. If there is anything I can do...,"

"I'll be all right. I just need a few minutes to push this to the back of my brain with all the other lousy calls and memories." She picked up the monitor and trauma bag and carried them to ALS 13. "CJ, do you mind cleaning the monitor while I restock the supplies?"

"No problem."

Silently the medics readied the truck to go back in service. By 5:30 the unit was spotless, fully stocked, and set for the next job.

"ALS 13's available," said CJ to the dispatch.

"Received ALS 13; available at 1730," dispatch replied.

"Ya know for such a slow day it sure got busy," Kendall said.

CJ laughed. "No predicting this business. Do you have to work tomorrow?"

"Nope, and I'm not in again until Thursday."

"Lucky you. I get to come back here bright and early," said CJ. "Oh my gosh! I forgot to tell you about Dr. Garrison."

"What?" Kendall asked.

"Well he followed me out to the rig and started asking me questions about the death of his maid. He wanted to know if she really killed herself with heroin."

"I'm surprised Mike told him anything yet."

"Me too, so I asked him where he heard that and he said 'from the press.' " CJ tapped her nails on the table.

"The press? How the heck did they get a hold of it so soon? I wonder if Mike knows?"

"That's his problem," snapped CJ. "I haven't told you the best yet. Garrison pretty much threatened my job if I didn't tell him what I knew."

"Get out of town," said Kendall.

"Yup. He informed me that he was indirectly my boss so I should tell him."

"Did you?"

"No way. I told him it would be a breach of patient confidentiality and that he was putting me in an uncomfortable position. So..." CJ grinned.

"Go on," said Kendall.

"So I gave him Trooper Garcia's work number," She made a silly face. "Let Mr. Big Shot take care of him."

"Good job."

"Actually I'm not sure where it would have gone if you hadn't pulled in with the patient and taken his attention away from me." She shook her head. "He was pushing for something, but I'm not sure what."

"Think he's involved with her death?" asked Kendall.

"Maybe," said CJ. "I'll sniff around some more tomorrow."

"I guess I'll spend my day off schmoozing the medical examiner for information."

"Not if mister tall, blonde and drop-dead gorgeous calls you tonight."

"Either way I'm still going to the ME's office."

"Hey take him with you. He can get the attention of Bob's snaggle-toothed secretary while you slip into his office and smooch. Sorry I mean schmooze with him."

"Very funny, and you could be right about old snaggle tooth. I think her bite is much worse than her bark. Officer Black might come in handy, considering I don't think she's had a date since the seventies."

Kendall hit the garage door opener.

"I sure hope we don't get a late job. I'm whipped," said CJ.

Putting it in reverse, Kendall backed the suburban into the garage. "I second that motion," said Kendall. "I'm looking forward to a tall ice-filled glass of coke and a hot bath."

"I thought you were trying to cut down on the soda," scolded CJ.

"I've tried. I think I need to form a self-help group to get off the stuff." Kendall laughed. "Hey if a glass of cola is my vice then I'm doing pretty good."

"You left out men," said CJ, smartly.

"I think I'd have an easier time swearing off those. Soda has never broken my heart or left me stranded at the drive-in."

"When did you get stranded at a drive in?" exclaimed CJ.

"Wouldn't you like to know," said Kendall, hopping out of the driver's seat. "Come on, let's finish up the paperwork and pray our relief shows up on time."

Surprise registered on the night medics' faces when they walked through the door at 18:45 to find CJ and Kendall talking and smiling!

"You two worked together today?" asked Bert.

"Yup," said CJ.

"Is the truck still standing?" said Joe.

"Stocked and ready to roll on the twenty-five jobs you're gonna get tonight," said Kendall.

"Very funny Rose, and I'll make sure I call you every time the pager goes off." Bert held out his hand for the keys to ALS 13. "Ya know, just to keep you informed."

"Gonna be a little hard to reach me if my phone's shut off," said Kendall. She smiled, dropping the keys into his open palm.

"Oh we'll find a way. Remember the medic motto: Adapt and overcome," said Joe. He held open the door. "Now get out of here and enjoy your night."

The women walked out to their cars together.

"Maybe pigs can fly," said Kendall.

"What the heck are you talking about?" asked CJ.

"Oh nothing. It turned out to be a good day, that's all."

CJ paused beside her car, then came over to Kendall and gave her a hug. "Thanks for giving me a chance. I had a good day, too."

Kendall patted her back. "Give me a call if you find anything out tomorrow."

"I'll call you either way. Maybe we can set up a lunch date to talk things out?"

"Maybe," said Kendall. She opened her car door and got in. "See ya later."

CJ pushed the Firebird's door shut and waved. "See you."

Nineteen

Route 80 traffic was a miserable blend of stop-and-go drivers and blatant idiots weaving in and out between cars. Her mood was sour, and it was nearly eight when she finally turned the Firebird onto the winding drive, leading to the twenty-acre estate where she rented the top floor of a beautiful, old Victorian. Once painted white with pink trim, it had served as the home of an affluent family in Warwick, New York. Now the paint was faded and cracking, sadly in need repair.

Years earlier it was converted into four apartments, two on the top floor and two on the bottom. Kendall lived on the top floor and immediately below her lived Tom Park. The other apartments remained vacant.

Kendall had formed a strong bond with Tom when she moved in shortly after her parents' deaths five years ago. Kendall, Tom, Bela, and Max had become a kind of surrogate family, going through the ups and downs of life together.

She parked the car next to her apartment's entrance, frowning because the stupid porch light was out again. A nasty wind shook the Formula Firebird, whipping a cold light rain into her face as she opened the door. Squinting her eyes against the rain she scanned the doorway, surprised to see something on the steps.

She grabbed the knapsack from the seat and quickly ran up the steps. Reaching down, she picked up a single, red rose and card. It was freezing cold as she slipped the key into the lock and turned it with her numb hand.

The door swung open freeing a large, yellow, slobbering ball of fur. Paws the size of a lions smacked her shoulders, knocking her off the steps onto the wet grass. She struggled to get up to no avail, covered by a hundred pounds of loving.

"Bela!" she cried, hugging the squirming dog, cooing sweet words into her ear. Forgetting the weather she rolled to her side and got up. "Come on girl, let's go!"

They took off into the darkness running past the Firebird and into the field beside the driveway. Bela ran in the rain, snapping at the drops while Kendall headed for cover in the old, red barn.

"Good girl," she shouted. "Hurry up and go! I'm freezing."

Bela obliged and a few minutes later they ran up the stairs, dripping water onto the wooden steps.

"Watch it girl. Don't slip. I can't afford another vet bill." Lovingly, Kendall pet the dog's head at the top landing.

Max, the tomcat, sauntered into the kitchen meowing loudly. He'd been part of the Montague clan for six years when she rescued him from the streets of Paterson. Starving and emaciated, Max had slowly grown stronger under Kendall's loving care.

Purring, the fifteen-pound, orange tabby swirled his body between Kendall's feet, rubbing against her legs. She bent down, petting him on his head. "Maxie, how's my boy?"

"Come on you two. I'll fix you some dinner and then I'm taking a hot bath!"

Bela gobbled down her food. Maxie ate with the dignity of a king while Kendall leisurely drank a cup of hot, strawberry tea and nibbled on buttered toast. The small apartment filled quickly with the scent of rose bath water steaming out from the running tub.

Sitting at her small kitchen table she gazed out the round turret windows looking over the back yard, and thought back on the strange day she had. She couldn't remember a shift quite as eventful. Today a definite step toward healing between her and CJ had happened, and for that she was glad. She had missed her friend. Would she ever be able to trust her again was the big question, and one she could not answer right now.

And then there was Mike. Why was a state trooper handling a local investigation? She picked up her cup of tea and walked into the bathroom with Bela and Max trailing behind her.

Setting the cup on the tub sill, she found herself reminiscing about how she first met Mike. It had been on a serious motor vehicle accident like today's. Then her patient had been a boy of seventeen, entrapped in a badly damaged Camaro.

She and CJ had split to handle multiple patients, and Mike had become her right hand on the call, not leaving her side until they had the boy out. She smiled, remembering how he had tracked her down later that day to see how the boy was doing. They both knew if a trooper was so concerned all he had to do was pick up a phone and call the hospital. Instead he came   to headquarters pretending to be all business.

Mike was six foot with a body to die for. They stood outside in shy silence until he finally suggested they sit in his cruiser for a while to "discuss the case."

His deep blue eyes had jumped out at her from his deeply tanned complexion. She found her mind wandering, wondering how he fit his incredibly toned body into the cruiser. Let's face it, he made her knees go weak.

She was thrilled when shortly into their conversation he asked her out, and pleasantly surprised when after dating for a few months he confessed to being as nervous as a school kid when he asked her for a date

She turned off the water, thinking how different her life would be if she'd just said no.

Unbuttoning her uniform shirt she slipped it into the hamper, following it with the rest of her clothes. Everything needed a good washing in hot water, but that could wait for tomorrow. She was beat.

Lowering one foot into the bubble bath, warmth crept up her body. Sitting down in the hot water, she heard her cell phone ring. "Oh bother," she said. Stepping out of the tub, she walked naked into the kitchen with Bela and Maxie on her heels. "Now who could this be you guys?"

Grabbing the phone from her bag, she glanced at the caller ID and smiled when she saw the name. Walking back to the tub of bubbles, she hit send. "Hello."

"Hello Kendall. This is Johnnie from Willow Run."

"Hey Johnnie, how are you?" Stepping back into the tub, she let out a sigh as her stiff muscles sank into the hot water. Max jumped up on the toilet seat purring loudly. Bela curled up on the bath rug in front of the tub, happily chewing on a peanut butter rawhide bone.

"Hope I didn't catch you at a bad time."

She smiled deliciously. "Not at all."

"Is that water I hear splashing in the background?"

"It is." She leaned her body against the soft pink bath pillow. "As we speak I am soaking in a bath filled with rose water. It's just what I needed after the day I had." She heard him exhale deeply. "Is everything all right Officer Black? You don't need a paramedic do you?" she said smartly.

"If she's you and she's covered only in bubbles," he groaned softly, "then I sure do."

"I'll be right over. Just as soon as I dry off."

He laughed. "Oh that's no fun. Come on now; give a guy a break. I've had a rough day, too."

Kendall turned serious. "Do you know anything more about the DOA?"

"Honestly, the staties are being real closed mouth about this one. Needless to say, it rankles those of us on the force."

"I was wondering about that. Why are the state police involved in the investigation at all?"

He cleared his throat. "Beats me. All I know is we got there and started the scene investigation and next thing you know, our chief is all pissed off and telling us to hand over the case to the state troopers."

"The chief didn't say why?"

"No, and Chief Fitzgerald is pretty tough. The only way he'd give up a scene to the state is if he was ordered to by someone higher up."

"Who would have that much pull?"

"I don't know. But I'm sure going to find out."

She sunk down lower into the water turning her neck from side to side to ease her tense muscles.

"Are you still there Kendall?"

"Sorry I faded off for a minute. Taking a bath makes me drowsy." She sat up exposing her breasts to the cold air. "Not that the company is boring."

Johnnie groaned. "To be company I'd have to be there." He swallowed loudly. "Which could be arranged if you give me an hour?"

"Now Officer Black, I thought you were working a double shift?"

"I am. But I think I'm starting to come down with a sore throat." He coughed. "Might be a twenty-four-hour bug."

"Don't tempt me," she said.

"That, my dear, is my very plan. To tempt you into seeing me again."

"Ya know." She splashed the water with her feet.

"I'm waiting with bated breath," whispered Johnnie.

"Well, it's just that I have some unanswered questions about the call, too." She cleared her throat softly. "Maybe we could work together and find some things out."

"Back to the cone of silence thing again."

"Well you did say I am agent 99."

"Oh no, we have to come up with a better code name then that. Let's see..,"

"So do we have a deal Johnnie?" she interrupted.

"Can I come over to continue this discussion after my shift ends at eleven?"

"You, Officer Black, are incorrigible."

"I most certainly am. So what do you say? I could be there around midnight."

Kendall hesitated. She only just met this guy. Did she really want him coming to her home so late? She reassured herself he was a cop. Then she remembered he was a cop. Cops were trouble with a capital T.

"That's a little too late for me; I'm really tired."

"How about 9:30 then. I won't stay long and I'll bring you a treat."

"What kind of treat?" She was beginning to soften. He was young and he was cute. And she was in need of a self-esteem boost after Mike today. "Any chance of a Cinnabon?"

"If I leave right now there is." She heard his keys jingling in the background. "So will it be a sore throat and Cinnabon, or will it be a lonely shift and a cold bath?"

Kendall laughed. "Do you like strawberry tea?"

"My favorite."

"I'll be waiting with bells on," she said.

"I hope that's all you'll have on."

"Officer Black, you have to promise to behave or the strawberry tea is off. We don't even know each other and I'm a bit old fashioned."

"I'm sorry. I didn't mean to make you uncomfortable. I was just kidding around."

Well that certainly knocked the wind out of her sail! As usual she was reading too much into his playful manner. After all,why would a young, gorgeous-as-heck guy be so interested in her. Face it, the guy looked like a bronze Adonis. He could have any woman he wants.

Geez Kendall, get a grip. Maybe he does like you. The question was, did she want to get to know him better or not. Sometimes it was hard being a woman. She dipped her shoulders below the water again.

"Sorry I didn't mean to read into things. I'd love to see you and your Cinnabon tonight." She laughed softly. "And it won't hurt to bring some extra cream cheese, too."

"Hold on. I'd better get out my notepad."

"Notepad! For what?"

"Do you have any milk?"

"Ah, no, I take my tea black."

"Didn't think so."

She heard him rustle the paper.

"What about candles?"

"Candles for what?"

"Do you or don't you?"

"Yes I have candles."

"Have you seen the new Dr. Doolittle movie yet?"

"What are you up to Johnnie?"

"Stick to the questions ma'am. Only the facts," he said, jovially.

"No I haven't seen the movie yet."

"Oh, and one more thing."

"Yes detective?"

"Are you involved with Trooper Garcia?"

"Excuse me?"

"I just want to know what my chances are with you. From what I saw today, you and he are or were involved." He inhaled sharply. "I guess what I want to find out is if there is room for me too. I don't want to make you uncomfortable. And I don't want to get hurt."

"Were. And I think so," she said softly

"Were is good. I was hoping for a little better than I think so." He whistled. "But I can live with that....for now." He sighed. "Not long ago I was involved in a relationship that ended abruptly, so I know what it's like to hurt. But life goes on. Doesn't it?"

"It sure does," said Kendall.

"See you around nine-fifteen."

"I look forward to it."

She hung up the phone. Slowly she washed her body with lavender soap, splashing water to rinse off. She stood up. The cool air felt good on her naked body and she softly chided herself when she found her mind wandering to Johnnie's hands caressing the coldness away. Whoa, take a step back sister. He's too young for you and you know it. Stop dreaming. He probably wants to have a fling with an older woman and send you on your way. Friends she thought. Yes that's what we'll be. Friends.

Twenty

He wondered if she'd gotten his little present. He hoped it would be all it takes to make her forget sticking her pretty little nose into his affair. Oops, former affair. He thought back to the pronouncement. Cheona had looked so innocent lying there in her sexy, little teddy. But he knew the shrew she really was. Just like his mother! She didn't care whose feelings she stepped on to get her way. Bitch!

Enough about her. Someday he'd recreate the same scene with his mother's wiggly flesh poking out from a little, lacy teddy. Oh what fun it would be to watch her eyes light up with fear when she realized he was going to fill her blood with drugs and there was nothing she could do.

"You ugly, bratty, little boy." She'd hiss at him. "Untie your mommy and she will make you feel all better."

Yeah, all better. Sick bitch! Sooner or later she would be begging for his mercy. No woman would ever control him again. Never! Especially not a certain blonde paramedic. He didn't want to hurt her. Not really. "Keep out of it Kendall or you and your partner will end up like the others," he whispered softly. He scooped up his car keys from the table and began the drive to Warwick, New York.

Twenty-one

CJ Wagner, for all her wealth, was a lonely and unhappy girl. From childhood everything had been handed to her on a silver platter. In fact, she never had to work for a thing in her life, not even her medic certification.

Her father had seen to that by paying off influential people. Amazing that despite her failing several tests, she had somehow managed to be the valedictorian. Nothing too good for daddy's little girl.

Sometimes she hated him for that. Sometimes she loved him. Thank God she got Kendall as a partner. She showed her the ropes and never let her get away with her pretty little rich girl act.

"Do your job like the rest of us or get out," Kendall snapped during their second shift together when she'd peeked into a blood soaked rig as CJ stood outside, waiting for someone to clean it.

"OK sunshine. Like I said, get in there and do your job like the rest of us or get out." She pointed to the squad EMT and some fellow paramedics. "'Cause I assure you little, rich girl we ain't impressed."

CJ had felt all eyes on her and knew it was now or never to hold her own. "No problem Kendall. I was just taking a breather."

She grabbed the handle and hoisted herself in. One part of her wanted to cry. Another part of her wanted to say screw you dad; I'm doing this without your help. And the last part of her wanted to get her things from the medic unit and walk away from it all.

But she stayed and was she glad she had, No longer a spoiled little rich girl. How could she be when she had seen things no rich girls ever would.

Going on calls in the Christopher Columbus housing projects had been a stark jab of reality. She followed behind Kendall walking through hostile crowds, the only white faces in a sea of black. She wallowed in the urine-filled elevators, praying no one would jump them or try to steal the narcotics they carried. Pit bulls, shootings, stabbings, drugs, alcohol, and psychotic patients filled her shifts. She'd come into her own because of this job.

Yes, she still had the money, but now far more important, she had self-respect. Somewhere along the line, she'd gone from poor, little rich girl to one ass-kicking mama thanks to Kendall.

Then Mike had pushed her to betray her best friend and partner, and that was something she'd never forget. Now she had a chance to make things right and she was going to, no matter what the cost.

Her dad had some pull with the hospital board. Let's see what he can find out about Dr. Garrison, she thought. She picked up her blue neon phone and dialed the main floor of the house.

Twenty-two

He was early. He parked his '68 silver Corvette across from the Victorian's drive and waited. He'd give her a little more time to unwind. Besides, how could he explain how quickly he'd gotten here from work?

He revved the engine slowly. This baby could out run anything. She fit his personality more so than his other vehicle, a dark blue Chevy pickup.

He leaned back in the seat with his eyes closed, remembering how she loved taking rides with him into the country. He'd lower the top and run his hands through her long, blond hair flying wildly in the wind.

Sometimes when it would rain, they'd park in a field steaming up the windows with their lovemaking. The raindrops would hit the canvas roof, splattering down the windows.

Once they were caught by a local cop. She was all embarrassed, but he just showed the cop his badge. Those days were fun. He missed them. He missed her.

A car drove slowly up the road on his right side. It stopped at the Victorian's entrance. It was a black two-seater Mercedes, fancy as hell. From his perch he glimpsed the driver.

"What the...?" He flung the Vette into drive following the Mercedes up the narrow, gravel lane. Both vehicles arrived at the entrance to Kendall's apartment at the same time. He parked the car and got out.

The door to the Mercedes opened slowly, just in time for him to greet its driver. "We meet again Officer Black," he said.

"Trooper Garcia, is that you?" Black said in a mocking tone.

"It sure is son."

"Now come on Mike, I'm not that young."

"Too young for Kendall." Mike stood with his back to Kendall's door. "What are you doing here?"

Johnnie climbed out of the Mercedes and stood in front of Mike. He was five ten with a lean, muscled body, compared to Mike's six foot bull of a frame. "Kendall and I have a date."

Mike shook his head. "You are mistaken."

"Oh really?" Johnnie bent down to pick up the Cinnabon box and movie. "Then why do I have with me her favorite and I might add, specially requested dessert?"

Neither of them noticed the door swing open, nor the angry blonde standing on the porch. Bela rushed past her down the steps. "What's going on here?"

Startled, the two men faced her. Bela took the opportunity to leap up soundly planting her muddy paws on Mike's blue jean jacket.

"Hello Bela. Good to see you girl." He knelt on the soggy grass, letting the enormous yellow dog lick his face. "I see you were expecting me at least."

"Expecting you?" said Kendall.

"Didn't you get the card I left you?"

"Card?" Kendall said, confused. Then it hit her. There had been a white envelope. What had happened to it when Bela knocked her down? "Did it come with a rose by any chance?"

"Yes," He pointed to the step. "I left them right there."

Scanning the grass, she walked to the edge of the gravel and picked up a dirty, rained-soaked envelope. She held it up. "Think I found it. She started to rip it open. "Gee Mike, I'm sorry. Bela knocked it out of my hand when I got home. I forgot all about it when..."

He grabbed the card from her hand and shook his head. "Forget it. You obviously have made other plans," he said stomping away. He lowered his body into the Vette and started the engine.

Leaning out the window he tipped his black cowboy hat and said to Johnnie, "May the best man win.." The sports car kicked up a trail of gravel as he floored the gas and left.

Twenty-three

Johnnie walked to her side. "What was that all about?"

"I don't know. He took the card before I could read it." She frowned. "I haven't heard from him in over a year and now he shows up on my doorstep."

She glanced up. The storm was getting nastier by the minute, keeping time with her mood.

He held the box out in front of him. "I've got something that might make you feel better."

She smiled and took the buns, flicking rain drops off the plastic top. "Follow me." She slapped her leg once and yelled, "Bela, come!"

Obediently, the dog dropped something from her mouth and sat touching her side to Kendall's leg. "Good girl. In we go." She pointed up the steep stairwell.

The three of them mounted the stairs, Bela beating everyone by a long shot.

At the top landing, Johnnie stroked the dog's soft fur. "I've got some goodies for you too, Bela." He held up a bubble gum-flavored rawhide. "Can I give it to her?"

"I'm mighty impressed Mr. Black. Why that's her favorite."

Dusting the floor with her sword-like tail, Bela sat trembling with excitement, waiting for the release command.

"Huff, Huff," barked the yellow lab.
Kendall smiled, holding her pointer finger up, and then dropped it quickly. "OK."

Greedily, the dog snatched the bone from Johnnie's hand and ran into the living room. The two humans followed.

"Well this is my humble abode," said Kendall. She set the box down on the kitchen table, next to two mugs, and went to put the water on for tea. Arms gently wrapped around her waist. She turned around. "You promised to behave yourself."

He cupped her chin in his large hand. Green eyes stared into hers. He bent his head, brushing his lips against hers, deepening the kiss pressing his body against hers.

"Johnnie." A knocked sounded on the outside door. Slipping out of his arms, she ran down the stairs, startled to see the face staring at her through the dark window. She pulled open the door. "Dr. Garrison. What are you doing here?"

Twenty-four

He pushed his way in, shutting the door behind him. "I'm here to talk to you about the call at my house this morning."

She felt something cold brush up against her arm.

"All you have to do is answer some simple questions and then stop the pressure from the board of directors."

Kendall backed away. "I don't know anything about pressure being put on you. As for answering questions, you already know I can't." She eased her body toward the stairs, relaxing when she noticed Johnnie's shoe, sticking out from behind the door. Good, he was listening.

Garrison reached out and grabbed her arm roughly. "I just want to talk to you." He released his grip. "Please."

"Why are you so intent on questioning CJ and me?" She nodded, when his face flashed a look of surprise. "Did you really think she wouldn't tell me about you cornering her in the rig?"

"I did nothing wrong." He moved his face to within inches of hers, exhaling. His breath stunk from stale smoke, causing her to recoil.

"Answer my questions or I assure you I will see to it you no longer work as a paramedic in the state of New Jersey!"

"Threaten me all you want Garrison. I'm not afraid of you." She shoved him away with her hand. "Stay out of my face or I'll call the cops. Then we'll see who won't be working."

His face filled with anger as he reached back to strike her with his hand. "Nobody talks to me like that."

A burning sensation shot through her face as his fist connected soundly with her left cheek.

"You son of a bitch!" A figure shot past Kendall knocking Garrison to the floor. "Call the cops I'll take care of him," said Johnnie.

Garrison fell, prostate with Johnnie landing on top of him. Officer Black pulled a pair of handcuffs from his jacket pocket and slapped them on the doctor's wrists. "You are under arrest for assault and battery."

He pulled the doctor to his feet and threw him against the wall. "Don't move one muscle or I'll take matters into my own hands." He looked up the stairs at Kendall on the phone. "Why are you so intent on finding out what happened today Dr. Garrison? Did you have something to do with it?" Garrison hung his head. "No. I had nothing to do with it." Tears dripped to the floor. "My son, my son..."

Shock registered on his face as pain shot through the base of his neck. "Why?" Johnnie lowered the unconscious man to the floor, shouting up the stairs - "Kendall you better ask for a rig too. The good doctor just fainted."

Twenty-five

Lt. Andy Grey of the Warwick, New York police department held his finger over the opening to the oxygen mask. The bag filled with the life-saving medicine as he slipped it onto the patient's face. "Tell me again what happened." He looked over at Kendall taking a blood pressure on the doctor's right arm.

"He showed up at my door asking questions about a call I was on earlier today at his home." She held up her finger to silence the room. "Blood pressure's elevated 230/120. You have medics coming right?"

Grey nodded. "Then what happened?" He knelt down checking Garrison's carotid pulse. "His pulse is strong, racing like crazy."

"The call I referred to, was one on which his live-in maid was found dead." Kendall motioned for Grey to hand her his pen. "Without breaking patient confidentiality, I can tell you things on the call did not make sense to my partner and me."

She wrote down the vital signs on a piece of notepaper. "Let's put it this way Lt. Grey. Have you ever in your career had a patient kill themselves by injecting heroin?"

"I've had lots of heroin overdoses." He fished his hand into the doctor's pocket and pulled out his wallet.

"Did one ever leave a computer-generated suicide note?"

Grey's face registered interest. "No. Never."

"He's vomiting. Let's roll him," said Kendall.

Grey and Johnnie grabbed the doctor's legs and torso. Kendall supported his head and pulled the non-rebreather oxygen mask off his face. "He's having one major hypertensive crisis," she said.

The doctor heaved a dinner of chicken soup onto the floor. "What the hell is this?" said Grey. He pulled a revolver out of Garrison's waistband. He shot Kendall a sympathetic look. "It appears you are one lucky lady."

Her face fell. "He could have killed me if you weren't here Johnnie."

"Doesn't look good," said a New York paramedic walking up the steps. "Are you a nurse?" he asked Kendall.

"No. I'm a Jersey medic." She handed him the sheet of vital signs. "He collapsed after he tried to assault me. Officer Black." She pointed to Johnnie kneeling at Garrison's feet. "He restrained the man while I called for help. You can tell them what happened next Johnnie."

The medics set up their equipment listening to Johnnie tell them about Garrison's collapse.

"No trauma involved?" asked the second medic.

"Nothing more than being restrained by these until backup arrived." He held up a pair of shiny silver cuffs. "I took them off when he went unconscious."

"Did you have to use any force to restrain him?" asked Grey.

"Not really." Johnnie slowly stood up. "I did have to push him off Kendall. He fell to the floor and I landed on top of him."

"He struck you Ms. Rose?"

"Yes Lt. Grey." Kendall stood up allowing the medics room to work. "If Officer Black hadn't stopped him I don't know what he would have done to me. I've never seen someone with so much rage."

The medic nodded. "I'm going to sedate him and tube him." He handed her a bag valve mask. "Could you set this up and be ready to ventilate him?"

She took the bag valve mask from him. "Sure, just let me know when." She turned back to Lt. Grey. "Garrison was agitated about something. I just wish I knew how he fit into the maid's death." She glanced over at Johnnie. "Did he say anything to you before he passed out?"

"No. Nothing," said Johnnie, flatly.

He sounded evasive to Kendall. What's he hiding? She looked over at Lt. Grey who was busy writing his report, thankful he didn't seem to notice.

"OK I need you to bag now ma'am," said the medic. He held onto the breathing tube sticking out of Garrison's mouth.

Kendall kneeled down and secured the bag valve to the end of the endotracheal tube. She compressed the oxygen filled bag with her hands squeezing once every five seconds. Garrison's chest lifted with each breath.

Together the group put Garrison on the stretcher then wheeled him to the ambulance.

Twenty-six

Garrison was on his way to Good Samaritan Trauma Center. Lt. Grey asked a few more questions and left with the promise to follow up if he had any more.

Johnnie was busy fixing tea in the kitchen as Kendall sat on the living room floor cradling Bela on her lap. Bela, her strength in hard times, looked up with concern in her big, brown eyes. Maxie the cat settled on her lap, too, edging out the yellow dog who graciously made room for her friend.

"It's OK girl." She stroked the dog's soft fur. "You did real well tonight. You didn't get in anybody's way. Good girl." She kissed the top of the dog's head.

"You too Max. Good boy." The tomcat purred with each stroke of Kendall's hand.

She leaned back, holding the ice pack Johnnie had given her onto her left cheek. It throbbed. She assured everyone she was all right and didn't need to go to the hospital. But if it was this bad in the morning she'd go.

"Do you want sugar?" called Johnnie from the kitchen.

"Stevia please."

"Stev-a what?" said Johnnie peeking his head around the doorframe.

Kendall rolled Bela and Maxie off her lap and stood up. "It's an herb that doesn't have many calories or cause a rise in blood sugar," she said, walking into the kitchen with eight paws following.

"Oh of course," said Johnnie sarcastically.

She punched his arm. "Keep it up dork and you'll need a rig too."

He grabbed his arm and feigned pain. "You win. You win."

She set the ice pack on the counter and reached up taking the herb container out of the cabinet. "Just a pinch will do of this stuff. It is pretty sweet." Suddenly the day caught up to her and she found herself fighting back tears. She looked down focusing on her tea.

Johnnie came to her side and put his arm around her shoulder. "You all right? How's the face?" He squeezed her lightly. "Are you sure you don't want to go to the ER? I'll drive you."

"Thanks. I'll be fine once this day is over." She looked into Johnnie's green eyes. "Will you answer a question for me?"

His face grew serious. "Yes, of course."

"I have the feeling you weren't telling Lt. Grey everything that went on tonight."

He leaned back against the cabinet and took a sip of peppermint tea. "You are very perceptive Ms. Rose." He set the tea down. "I was going to tell you everything over a cup of tea."

She sipped her strawberry tea. "I took a sip and so did you," she said, cocking her head. "So spill it officer."

Johnnie smiled at the strong-willed blonde. "Well right before Garrison collapsed I asked him if he was involved in the maid's death. The guy started to cry. The last words he said were 'my son, my son.' "

He looked down at Bela curled up at Kendall's feet. "Real nice dog you have there." He leaned down petting the dog with his free hand. Maxie strolled over rubbing against Johnnie's ankles. "Meow."

Johnnie laughed. "Yes you're a good kitty too." His large hand petted the tomcat gracefully.

Kendall smiled, relieved he'd come clean with her. "So what do you make of that?"

"I don't know. But I'm sure going to find out." He stood up and finished his tea with a deep sip. "I think you and I could make a good team."

"Team huh?" said Kendall.

He took the mug from her hand and set it down on the counter. "Come on, you should go to bed. I'll tuck you in." He led her down the hall then stopped. "Which way?"

She pointed to the last door on the left. "I need to change. Why don't you watch some TV?" Bela raced past Johnnie and jumped up on the king-sized bed.

He laughed. "Don't be long. Bela's built and she's good-looking too."

From the bathroom mirror, a red blotch jumped back at her. She gingerly touched her cheek. It didn't feel broken. Gently she washed off her makeup and moisturized her face. From jeans and a sweater she changed into a tee shirt and sweats. No time like the present for the handsome man to see her without makeup.

Looks had always been a big deal growing up. She'd never been judged by what she did.; always, how she looked.

Then the death of her parents had changed all that for her. She finally realized that being comfortable with herself was all that mattered, not how she looked or what she wore. To be real, to live life.

If someone didn't like the way she looked, then look somewhere else. She recited this to herself as she walked into the bedroom.

Johnnie sat on the bed propped up by two large pillows, one sage green and the other pastel pink. Each had a large flower in the middle. "Hey gorgeous," he said. Bela lay stretched out along his right side. He patted the bed. "Come sit by me."

She walked to the bed then crawled over Bela and Johnnie. Slowly he took her in his arms and kissed her softly.

"How's the face kiddo?" He touched her cheek. "Sorry honey. I wished I had been down there to stop him. I'm really sorry."

She gazed at him in wonder. "Johnnie you saved my life. If you hadn't been here..."

He sat back and pulled her body into his strong chest, kissing the top of her head. "Now I know you would like nothing more than to ravish my body young lady."

She snuggled closer.

He drew up her tee shirt exposing her back. "Unfortunately you will have to control yourself and let me give you the best back rub of your life." His gazed traveled around the room landing on a bottle of rose body crème. "This will do nicely." He picked up the lotion and squirted some onto his hands rubbing them together. "Now lay on your stomach please."

She sat up, teasing him with a glimpse of her breasts before she settled onto the bed face down. Strong hands kneaded her sore muscles. Sleep drifted to her slowly. She felt comfortable with this man. Her hero. How would she ever repay him for saving her life? Outside raindrops fell briskly, bouncing off the tin roof to the ground below.

Twenty-seven

Good Samaritan was busy tonight and Andy Grey was in no mood for it. He sat outside the prisoner's room watching the team working furiously to save his life. Grey didn't like the feel of this one. A renowned trauma surgeon assaults a paramedic over some maid. Come on, give him a break. What the hell really happened back there and who wasn't telling the truth?

Black seemed like a credible witness. The medic seemed like she was hiding something. He smiled at a cute red-head nurse walking by him into Garrison's room. Hey, at least the scenery wasn't bad.

He jumped up as the doors to Garrison's room shot open. The team wheeled the good doctor's gurney past him at breakneck speed. He caught up to the red head. "Where are you taking him?" he asked.

She shot him a look. "He's got a bad head bleed. We have to get him to the OR for emergency surgery." She squeezed down on the bag valve mask sending precious air to Garrison's lungs."

"What are his chances?"

"To put it bluntly, he's a dead man, or worse, a vegetable if the surgery doesn't work. Does he have any family you can contact?"

Grey looked down at his notes. "Yes, a wife and two sons." He stopped short at the doors to the OR. The team rushed by him. "I'll call them now," he shouted to the retreating forms.

What had precipitated this whole mess he didn't know, but he was damn well gonna find out. Back at the nurse's station he picked up the phone and dialed.

Twenty-eight

The shrill ring of the phone at 7:30 jolted Kendall awake. She fumbled for the receiver beside her bed running into a large man hugging a hundred pound lab-mix, who looks suspiciously like Bela.

She sat up rubbing her eyes. The day before came back to her. It wasn't a dream after all.

Leaning over Johnnie, she grabbed the phone and said in her best morning voice, "Hello."

"Hi Kendall. It's CJ."

She stretched over the top of Johnnie who grabbed her body hugging it to his. "Hey you. Cut that out!" she scolded sweetly.

Johnnie's luminescent green eyes opened and he smiled. "Well good morning to you too gorgeous."

"What did you say Kendall?" asked CJ. "Is someone there with you?"

Kendall laughed into the phone. "You might say that girl friend." She rolled off Johnnie and playfully struck him with a pillow.

He feigned injury. "I think I need a paramedic."

"Kendall Rose, is that who I think it is?"

"If you mean tall, blonde, and handsome. Yes."

"You lucky girl you." CJ laughed. "So..."

"So nothing happened except Garrison showed up with a gun, assaulted me, was wrestled to the ground by Johnnie, and is now admitted to Good Samaritan with a head bleed."

Johnnie got up. "Coffee, tea, or me?" he said.

"Tea please," said Kendall, holding the phone away from her face. "CJ's stuttering."

CJ coughed. "I had my dad do some checking on Garrison."

"That explains what he said."

"Said what?" said CJ.

"For me to stop putting pressure on him," she snorted. "Like I have any connections."

"I feel bad now. I only wanted to help."

"You didn't cause this to happen. He came up here on his own. Right before he collapsed he implicated one of his sons in the death of Cheona Carpenter."

"You're kidding. Isn't one the fire chief we worked with yesterday at the wreck?"

"The very one running the extrication on my vehicle," said Kendall. "That makes it all the more unfortunate that Garrison collapsed before we could get anything else out of him."

Johnnie handed her a steaming cup of English breakfast tea.

Kendall smiled. "Thank you."

"Well that proves something isn't on the up and up with the girl's death." said CJ.

"That's how I feel too. We can't stop until we find out what happened. Johnnie must know the son if he's chief."

Johnnie cleared his throat.

Kendall looked up. Johnnie's handsome face was frozen in a menacing scowl.

"We have to talk," said Johnnie. He motioned to the phone. "Please tell her you'll call her back."

Kendall frowned. "CJ, Johnnie wants to talk to me. I'll call you back later after my visit to the Medical Examiner's office."

She hung up. "What's wrong Johnnie?"

Johnnie paced the room. "I don't want you and CJ involved in this any further. You aren't law enforcement."

"Last night you were all for us working together. What happened?"

"Garrison happened. That's what."

"He's in the hospital. He can't hurt us anymore. I doubt he's gonna be out anytime soon, if ever."

"I don't care." Gently he touched her bruised cheek. "Please let me handle this."

"Oh, so suddenly you have connections with the ME's office."

He shot her a smug look. "I have far deeper connections than you'll ever know."

She squinted at him. "Of course, your last name's Black. How stupid of me." She held her hands up. "So what are you doing slumming with the likes of an underpaid paramedic?"

His frown disappeared. "That's not what I mean."

Kendall edged her way off the bed and stood up to face him. "Why don't you tell me what you meant then Johnnie Black?"

Bela growled softly. Maxie jumped off the bed running out of the room.

He pulled her into his arms crushing her against his broad chest. "Honey, I am so sorry I came off like a snob. I didn't mean to insinuate anything." With his hand, he lifted her chin. "I just don't want anything to happen to you. I think we're at the start of something good."

She pressed her hands into his chest and leaned back. "Then let's get something straight, right from the get go. I can take care of myself. I have since my parents died. And I don't like someone telling me what I can and cannot do. If you have concerns, then we can discuss them. But no orders."

Johnnie stepped back and studied her. "You know for a skinny blonde you sure are one tough chick." He grabbed her hand and shook it. "OK, you got a deal." He smiled. "Sorry," he said meekly.

"Oh dear, our first fight," she said sarcastically. Grabbing his hand she pulled him out to the kitchen for breakfast.

Johnnie pushed his chair back from the table and glanced at this watch. "I'm starting four to twelve's today. I'd best be going." He rose then stood before her. He held out his hand.

Kendall placed her hand in his and stood up. She wrapped her arms around his waist as he pulled her to his chest. "Thanks for being there for me last night."

He kissed her softly on the lips. "I'll be here for you every night if you'll let me."

She smiled. "Time will tell young buck."

He rolled his eyes. "Are you still set on going to the medical examiner's office today?"

She shook her head yes.

"Nothing I can do to change your mind?"

"Nope." She reached up and touched his lips lightly with her fingers. "First I'm going to the gym, then the

shooting range to practice for a bit. I like to keep sharp."
She patted the holstered Glock on the table. "You never
know when you're going to need to use it. I'll call you
when I'm done."

"Ah, a regular Annie Oakley." His shoulders slumped.
"Sorry I can't go with you. It's too late for me to call out.
We're really short staffed."

Kendall kissed him deeply. She felt his arousal press
against her abdomen. Lowering her hands she cupped his
hard butt, pressing her body tightly against him. Her
breathing deepened, keeping time with her racing
heartbeat.

His breath caught. "Whoa baby. Keep this up and we
both won't be going anywhere."

Letting him go she stepped back. Her skin flushed
with heated arousal. "You are so sexy Johnnie."

Johnnie scooped up his keys breathing heavily.
"What you do to me Ms. Rose." He winked then trotted
down the stairs

Twenty-nine

By eight fifteen, she was behind the wheel of the Firebird, heading to the gym in Wayne. Tapping her fingers on the wheel, she thought about her good friend Bob Crosby, who had recently been promoted to head honcho. When she called him, out of the blue, he was thrilled to hear from her and more than happy to let her watch Cheona Carpenter's autopsy, set for 1:30 today. She'd be there in an unofficial capacity of course. She hummed softly to herself. They'd get to the bottom of this, one way or the other. She hoped CJ had some luck with the nurses too.

She turned left, onto route ninety-four. If traffic's light, she'd make it in under an hour. Today her mind was not in the moment, for if it were she would have seen him. Waiting, watching.

Thirty

He stood across the street, concealed by heavy brush and trees, eating a bagel with cream cheese. Leaning against a huge oak tree, he laughed out loud thinking about the reaction he'd have the pleasure of seeing shortly.

The bitch is going to come out on the porch and start screaming her head off. He thought of the rat's bulging red eyes, its body contorting as he strung it through the porch rafters. Good thing rats can't yell for help. Pitiful creatures, really.

He watched the Victorian's side door open. Rubbing his hands together, he waited anxiously for her to see it. His face froze mid-giggle as he watched the blonde walk down the steps smiling.

What the hell had happened? She should have found it! She should have run screaming down the steps. Only she wasn't. The damn bitch was simply walking to her piece of crap car. Damn it, why can't things ever be simple?

He fingered the gun strapped to his side. Now this would be simple. Simple and yet so unfulfilling. Melting against the tree, he waited for the air-polluting Firebird to turn out of the driveway.

The aging, blue, muscle car sat idling at the end of the road. Balling his fists he froze, flattening his agile body against the tree. Had she seen him? Why wasn't she leaving?

Slowly the rusted Firebird turned left onto the main road. Relief, mixed with arrogance, as he spat on the muddy ground.

What had he been thinking? there was no way she'd seen him. One thing he learned from dear, old mom, was no woman was very observant. Hell, they could barely chew gum and walk at the same time.

Scanning the surrounding area from his hiding spot, he slowly made his way through the wooded area to his dark car hidden down the road. Slipping behind the wheel, he jammed the key into the ignition, starting the powerful engine with a twist of his manicured hand.

Putting the car in drive he drove slowly from the woods. No need to draw attention, especially since he decided to leave her another little present, one that will wipe that smirk off her face. His lips twisted into a sneer. Hell, why waste the trip? This time it will be something bigger than a dead rat. Let's see, what rhymes with rat...

Thirty-one

"So, Dr. Garrison was worried about something?" said CJ.

Cheryl Lane, a registered nurse for two years, nodded back. "Yeah, for the last month or so he's really been on edge, snapping orders at us, like we were his own personal servants or something."

She picked up a syringe and jabbed it into a medication vial. "Seemed to have something to do with his son." She tapped the needle, releasing air bubbles back into the vial. "What was his name now?"

"Isn't it Jack? Jack Garrison." said CJ.

"Yup. That's it." She brushed by CJ. "Sorry I can't talk anymore." She shook the syringe. "Time to give Mr. Milton his daily shot of B-12."

CJ thanked her for her help. At the nurses' station she spotted a nurse she'd known for several years. "Hey Rhonda," she said to the short brunette.

Rhonda looked up in surprise. "Hi CJ. I haven't seen you in ages."

CJ smiled. "I'm working as a medic now."

Rhonda smiled. "Finally made something of yourself. I'm proud of you." She tapped her pen against her chin. "But from the look on your face, I'd say you have something else on your mind."

CJ nodded. "I was wondering if you know Dr. Mark Garrison."

"Sure I do," Patting a seat she motioned for CJ to sit down. "What's up?"

"I can't go into details because of patient confidentiality, but we had a call at his house. After the call, he kind of threatened me over something."

Rhonda gripped CJ's arm, leaning forward. "You're kidding me! He has been acting strange lately."

"How so?" asked CJ.

"Well the gossip around here is..." she paused, looking around the nurses' station for ease droppers. Leaning closer, she continued, "He was having an affair and it went sour. He turned into a real bastard. Always nasty to the nurses, screaming orders at us. That kind of thing."

"Do you know who the other woman is?"

Rhonda laughed. "You know me honey. I tried." Twirling her hands she leaned back in her chair. "He was worse than Fort Knox to break. My guess is a nurse on the fourth floor. He seemed to spend a lot of time there."

CJ thanked her and left. She bet the fourth floor was a dead end. She had a feeling it wasn't a nurse with whom he'd been having an affair. In the ER parking lot, her partner, Jerry Knight, sat in ALS 12, waiting to head out for lunch. She grabbed a quick hundred from the ATM in the lobby then headed out through the emergency room to the idling suburban.

Thirty-two

It was five after nine when she pulled into the gym lot, scanning the parking area for a space. Darn, it's pretty crowded for this time of the morning. Hope I can get my full work out in before I meet Bobbie, she thought.

In the far corner she spotted a narrow space next to a large, green pickup truck. Angling the Firebird partly on the grass, she slipped beside the truck, humming to herself as she got out.

Dressed in matching dark blue stretch shorts and tank top, she trotted into the lobby, waving to Sandy who was answering the phone at the front desk. She felt charged, ready for a good work out. Some days it was a struggle to get here, some days it wasn't. But, no matter how she felt for the past year since breaking up with Mike, she decided to make working out her top priority. She was so into it now, she was thinking about going back to school to get certified as a personal trainer. Why not earn some extra money on the side and keep in shape at the same time? A win-win proposition.

Strolling into the ladies locker room, she opened locker five and put her things into it, closing the door with a bang. Today she was going to do the upper body workout she designed for herself.

Gathering her long, blonde hair, she pulled it into a ponytail, securing it with a purple band, and then made her way into the work out area. Going to the free weights, she grabbed two ten-pound weights and two fifteen-pound weights, setting them down on a weight bench.

Placing a towel onto the bench she stood up stretching in the mirror. She didn't notice him, sitting at the machine behind her. Locking her hands, she stretched out her arms in front of her, glancing up in the mirror. Anger rolled up her limber spine as she stood, watching the little weasel's eyes rake up and down her body, with undisguised lust.

The guy looked well toned and muscled, with mousey brown hair and eyes to match. She'd never seen him at the gym before and wished she wasn't seeing him now. Maybe if she ignored him he'd just go away. Picking up a five-pound weight she started the first set.

Pulling down her arm into a tricep stretch, she glanced in the mirror again. The guy was still there and still staring at her. His eye closed in a wink, then opened allowing his gaze to slowly travel the length of her body.

So the twerp wanted to play games. Well this game was beginning to piss her off, since the reason she had picked this gym was it wasn't a meat market; it was a real gym where people actually came to work out.

Dropping her arm, she turned around and faced him. "Can I help you with something?" she said, sarcasm dripping from her mouth.

Mr. Weasel's face turned bright red and he began to mumble something in a stuttering fashion.

"What's that sir? I can't hear you?" she snapped.

"Uh, uh, sorry. I, I, thought I k...k...knew you from somewhere," he stammered. Standing up he ambled over to her. "W, w, were you, were you, by chance on a call in Willow Run yesterday?"

Looking him up and down, she said. "Who wants to know?"

He held out his small hand. "Th..th...the name's Gail Gas. I'm a sp....special officer for the Willow Run po...po...police department."

It was almost painful watching his mouth contort, as he tried to get his words out. To top it off his handshake was wimpy, cool, and sweaty. Gail Gas, she wanted to say, what's that some kind of windy fart. She wanted to, but she didn't. Instead she said, "Kendall Rose."

"I...I.... know who you are," He smiled, revealing gray, tobacco stained teeth. His breath smelled of stale coffee and cigarettes.

"Oh, were you at the scene?" She yanked her hand free from his sweaty hand. "I don't remember seeing you there," she said, wiping her hand on her shorts. She slowly stepped back from him.

"Ah, yeah, ah yeah, I, I, I was there. I'm a....a....assisting in the investigation."

"Assisting, huh. Good for you," She picked up a ten-pound weight. "Well, I guess I better get back to my workout. I don't have much time."

"Why don't, why do, do, don't you put that weight down and ta, ta, talk to me," he said, with authority.

Cocking her head, she gave the creep a once over. "Officer Gas, I don't mean to be rude, but like I said I need to get back to my work out. I have limited time today."

Stepping forward, he practically pinned her legs against the weight bench. "I....I just, I just, want to talk about the call," he said, saliva spraying her face.

Lifting her arms, she quickly pushed her hands against his broad chest. "Back up! Now!" she said, loudly. She didn't care what he did for a living, the guy was a certifiable whack job.

To her right, a massive frame put down two twenty five pound weights and cleared his throat.

Gail backed away, holding up his hand. "Just, just, just wanted to talk to her b...b....buddy. No, no problem here."

Kendall stepped backward over top the weight bench, putting it between her and the bulky cop. "What's your major malfunction Gas?" she said, angrily.

"No problem." Leaning against the full-length mirror he shot her a grin. "I heard you, you talking to the trooper in charge of the investigation. S...s...seems he doesn't believe your little theory."

Shrugging, she didn't reply.

"Wooo, would it interest you to, to know that I...I....I agree with you?"

Staring at him through venom filled eyes she said, "Whatever Officer Gas."

"Whatever?" he said, angrily. "She...she....she was murdered you know," he said with a devious smile. Pulling his five- foot-six frame into the air. "If, if, you want to talk to me about it, you bet.. better have a better, better attitude."

He handed her a pre-printed Willow Run police business card. "Ca...ca...call me."

When she hesitated to take it, he said - "G....go ahead. I won't bite." Slipping it into her hand he walked toward the men's locker room. Turning at the entrance he raised his hand in a mock salute. "Enjoy your, your work out, Paramedic Rose."

Watching him go, she suddenly felt unnerved by the man. Was the guy trying to be intimidating or help her in his own insane way?

"Are you OK?"

At the sound of a deep voice, her face shot up. Looking into the deep brown eyes of the man with the massive frame, she nodded. "I am now. Thanks for your help back there."

"My pleasure," he said.

"Do you know that guy?" she asked.

"I've seen him hanging around the gym. Pretty big for a guy who doesn't work out much. My guess is he's on roids."

Kendall raised her eyebrows. "Steroids? Well that would sure explain his sudden mood swings and aggression." She shook her head. "Man, a guy like that shouldn't be a cop."

"That little twerp's a cop?" said massive man.

"Believe it or not, he's a special officer in Willow Run."

"Well, remind me to steer clear of Mr. Special," he said, laughing.

He has a good laugh, she thought. Holding out her hand she said, "My name's Kendall."

He reciprocated. "Hi, Kendall. I'm Marty," His grip was firm and confident.

"Thanks again. I've got to boogey if I want to get my work out in," said Kendall.

Marty smiled. "See you around."

By 10:30 she had showered, blow-dried her hair, and was applying the finishing touch to her eye makeup, outlining her blue eyes with dark brown, smoky shadow.

She liked the way she looked, finally now that she was in her forties. So many years of wasted energy feeling ugly and unsure. Better late than never, she thought.

Whistling, she grabbed her gym bag and walked outside to her Firebird. She would easily make it to the range with time to spare to stop at the 7-Eleven for two ice-cold diet Dr. Peppers.

The green pickup was gone, giving her a clear view of her car. A red rose jutted out from underneath the wiper blade. Attached to it was a plain, white card. "Call me" was written in blue ink.

What is it with men and roses lately? Glancing around the parking lot she scanned the area for the little steroid-popping creep. She threw the rose onto the ground and backed over it with the Firebird, leaving it mangled on the pavement.

Thirty-three

Arriving at the police shooting range promptly at 10:45 she parked the Firebird next to a nineteen-eighty, red Trans Am.

Lt. Bobbie Angel, a sharp shooter for Wayne police and her best friend, was warming up.

"Hey girlfriend," she called from the gate. "Ready to try and kick my butt?"

"Oh, I'll kick your butt. Just like last time sister," Kendall teased.

Having only been shooting for two years she knew she was no match for Bobbie.

For the past year the two women had a standing once-a-week shooting lesson. Bobbie, the long, curly blonde-hair instructor, and Kendall ,the willing student, made quite the striking pair and always garnered a small crowd of onlookers.

"What the hell happened to your face?" Bobbie lifted Kendall's chin with two fingers examining the bruise.

"Long story. I'll tell you later." Taking the Glock out of her purse, she faced Bobbie. "So teach, what's the lesson plan for today?"

Bobbie locked eyes with her student. "Sure you're OK?"

Kendall nodded.

She reached out and touched Kendall's arm. "In that case my friend, today is a free for all." Bobbie pushed in her earplugs and pulled down her safety glasses. "Come on, let's see what you're made of." She took aim firing off a round of bullets into a target at the far end of the outdoor shooting range. She didn't miss her mark.

"Like I can match that," said Kendall, following her lead with earplugs and safety glasses. Picking up the Glock she did a quick check of the weapon. Looking left and right, she assured herself the area was clear and took aim. Bullets flew through the air pummeling the paper outline of a man.

"Wow girlfriend. You mad at someone?" Bobbie walked out to the target. "I do believe you just succeeded in kicking my ass."

Kendall puffed out her chest and squared her shoulders. "Not bad for a rookie."

Bobbie shot her a look. "Seriously, this is the best you've ever shot." Bobbie cocked her head giving Kendall her standard what's up look.

Turning away from the target Kendall shrugged her shoulders.

Bobbie lifted her head and laughed. "Oh no. Not again."

"What?" said Kendall.

"He's back isn't he?"

"Who?"

Bobbie shook her head. "Don't play coy with me. I know you like the back of my hand. I haven't seen that look on your face since last year."

Kendall ran her fingers through her feathered hair. "Can't fool you can I?" Taking her place again she took aim and then lowered the gun. "I saw him yesterday, on a weird call."

Bobbie came to stand next to her putting her arm around her shoulder. "The call was weird or he was?"

"Both." Kendall turned, hugging Bobbie. "I feel like the wounds have been ripped open all over again."

"Ah honey. Tell me all about it."

"You mind if we just shoot for a bit first. I really want to get this practice in."

"Sure. You owe me lunch anyway."

Kendall laughed. "Ya think."

"I think." Bobbie went back to her station. "Ready?"

"Ready!" Kendall shouted.

An hour later the women put down their guns. They took off the safety equipment, packed up their weapons, and walked out to their cars.

"So coach, where do you feel like going?" Kendall swung open the door to the Firebird. "I have to go to an autopsy at 1:30."

"Autopsy? Yuck!" said Bobbie. "I can't wait for you to fill me in. How about Casey O'Tooles on Hamburg Turnpike?"

"Sounds good. See you there."

The Firebird Formula took the lead with Bobbie following in her candy-apple red Trans Am.

Thirty-four

Bobbie slid into the booth opposite Kendall.

"What took you so long? The old bucket of bolts give you a problem?" said Kendall.

Bobbie smacked the menu in Kendall's hand. "Ol' bucket of bolts, huh? And what exactly is that you pulled up in?"

"A classic of course," Kendall said, smartly.

Bobbie rolled her eyes. "That's right. I forgot. Your car's one year closer to being an antique, than mine."

The girls bantered back and forth easily as if they'd been friends since girlhood. The truth was they'd only met two years ago while teaching at the local police academy. Kendall teaching emergency care and Bobbie teaching fire arms. But their friendship wasn't cemented until a year later at the scene of a hostage situation. As members of the SWAT team, Bobbie had gone barreling in, with Kendall trailing behind her. While Bobbie rescued the hostage, Kendall tended to the shaken woman. Gradually, working together, Bobbie and Kendall had discovered they had a lot in common.

They referred to each other now as soul sisters, not of blood, but of choice. When Kendall was devastated by the betrayal and break up with Mike, Bobbie supported her with unconditional love. For the past year the women had become inseparable friends.

Although raised in different places, the women discovered many parallels in their lives. Both drove what they liked to call classic cars. Kendall's a 1979 Atlantis blue Firebird Formula and Bobbie's 1980 candy-apple red Trans Am with a fading silver bird on its hood. Both cars screamed for restoration; both women's pockets came out empty of extra cash.

Men, too, had come and gone in their lives with alarming frequency, until Kendall married at age thirty-two and Bobbie at age thirty-four.

But Kendall's marriage only lasted a mere five years while Bobbie, thankfully, was still happily married to Chris Angel, a cop from Sussex County.

"So what are you having?" asked Bobbie.

Kendall rested her chin on her hands. "I haven't had much of an appetite since Mike's reappearance." Picking up the menu, she said, "I guess a grilled mozzarella on whole wheat will do."

Bobbie glanced at her friend aware that she was hurting. "That bad, huh?"

Kendall shook her head. "I'm afraid so. My stomach's been in knots since I ran into him on a call. I never expected to see Mike again, much less have to do a pronouncement for him."

Bobbie shot her a look of surprise. "Come on now girlfriend. Your jobs are so intertwined. You didn't really believe that, did you?"

Kendall shrugged. "Wishful thinking I guess."

The waitress stood at the table, poised to take their orders. Kendall asked for a coke and grilled cheese. Bobbie, her usual green salad with tuna fish and house dressing. A shared plate of fries finished off the order.

Bobbie watched the waitress go. "So what are you going to do?" She leaned across the table. "I get the feeling you'd take him back in a heartbeat."

Kendall shook her head. "Actually, he asked me to talk and I turned him down."

116

Bobbie squeezed her hand. "Good for you. That man has hurt you enough."

Kendall sat back, staring into her friend's dark, green eyes. "I guess so." Needing a change of subject she raised her eyebrows and winked. "So how's that sexy man of yours?"

Across from her she saw Bobbie's eyes widen and a sudden twitch start at the corner of her full mouth.

"Bobbie, honey. What is it?"

Bobbie's eyes filled with water. "I think he's cheating on me."

"No way. Not Chris," said Kendall.

Bobbie shook her head. "Then you explain all the overtime he's working, with no money showing up in his check. I mean the dope doesn't remember I handle all the banking."

"Maybe he's taking comp time," Kendall said.

"Checked that out too." Bobbie leaned back in her seat, a frown on her strained face. "He's been using up his vacation and comp time like there's no tomorrow."

Kendall shook her head with disgust. "I thought he was one of the good guys." Placing her napkin on her lap, she looked up at Bobbie. "I thought you had the perfect marriage. It used to make me green with envy the way you two carried on like teenagers."

"I thought we had Camelot." Bobbie gazed out over the other patrons. "I guess I was blind. Hell, they say the wife's the last to know."

"Yeah, well, in this case the second to last. Because I sure as hell had no idea," said Kendall.

Both women looked up as the waitress arrived with their lunches. "Grilled cheese," she said.

Kendall raised her hand and the woman set it down in front of her. She did the same for Bobbie. "Anything else ladies?"

"No thanks," said Kendall.

Bobbie played with the salad using her fork. The waitress stood staring at her.

"Nothing for her either," said Kendall.

The waitress rolled her eyes, swishing her hips as she walked away.

"I sure as heck am tipping according to service today," spat Kendall.

"I never saw it coming," said Bobbie, lost in thought.

"So who is it?" asked Kendall.

Reaching in, Bobbie pulled a tattered, yellow piece of notepaper from her purse, and handed it to Kendall. "Take a look at what I found in his uniform pocket. He knows I take care of the dry cleaning. Hell, let's face it, I take care of everything while he goes on with his life like he's single."

Kendall read the hand-written love note, raising her eyebrows. "Who's Jill?"

Bobbie exhaled loudly. "His current partner."

"Oh no," said Kendall, sadly.

"Yup. None other," said Bobbie. She picked the note off the table and stuffed it back in her purse. "Why couldn't he just talk to me? I mean if there were problems, we could have worked them out."

"You sound as if it's already over."

Bobbie looked at her friend. "There are deal breakers and there are things you can work out." She tapped the table with her pointer finger. "And this, my dear, is a deal breaker."

Kendall nodded. "Still, maybe you should talk to him. You know, get his side of the story."

Bobbie stared at Kendall, as if she'd lost her mind. Then, slowly, a look of understanding crossed her face. "Maybe you could do that, but not me."

"Then I'm here to support you in whatever you do," said Kendall, reaching across the table to squeeze her friend's hand.

"In that case," said Bobbie, leaning in toward Kendall. "I've got something I'd like you to help me with."

Kendall smiled, hesitantly as she saw the expression on Bobbie's face.   "Ah, what do you have in mind?"

"Help me nail the bastard, in a way he'll never forget."

Thirty-five

In the far corner of the restaurant, hidden by the shadows, sat a lone man. From his vantage point he easily watched the two women engrossed in conversation. Damn, he should have sat closer; he couldn't hear a word they are saying. No, he thought, I can't take the chance of her spotting me. Maybe he should learn lip reading. It would come in handy right now. They both seemed agitated over something. Damn her for bringing in another cop, especially a woman.

Lost in fantasy, he didn't notice the short waitress standing in front of him, jutting out her pert, young, tits.

"Can I get you anything else sir?"

His head shot up, eyes locked on the bitch daring to interrupt him. "What?" he said sharply.

The brunette backed up, caught off guard by the sudden change of personality in the man who'd been flirting with her since he came in. "Sorry to bother you sir. I just wanted to see if you needed anything."

His eyes softened, taking in the stupid girl clutching a menu to her perky chest. He wanted to reach out and pull it down, along with the zipper on her skimpy shirt.

"Forgive me, my dear. I was lost in thought, over my sick mother." This shtick always worked. He laughed inside, as he watched the menu drop along with the fear on her face.

Leaning down she gave him amble view of her cleavage. So, she had lowered the zipper. This one was his for sure. She'd do for an afternoon of fun.

"Oh you poor baby."

He felt her hand run up and down his shoulder. His cock hardened, as he looked beyond her to the two blondes, imagining how their hands would feel on his toned body.

"U'm, you sure look yummy," he said, gazing up at the waitress.

Blushing, she leaned in closer, practically shoving her tits into his face. "I get off at four," she said, seductively pushing a napkin toward him.

He picked it up, glancing at numbers written on it. Winking, he said, "How about I pick you up at four?"

Excitement radiated from the girl's body. "Great."

Behind her he watched Kendall's eyes go wide. The blondes leaned closer together, whispering, conspiring. What the hell were they up to?

The waitress sighed. Was she still here? He looked up, dismissing her with a curt smile. "Later."

She stood there momentarily confused over the sudden change. "You'll pick me up at four?"

"Yeah, yeah four baby. I can hardly wait."

She smiled and trotted away. He watched her leave, knowing the girl had no idea what awaited her. Hell, if he couldn't have what he wanted right now, she'd do.

He shrugged his shoulders staring at Kendall and her cop friend. Leaving money on the table, he walked out briskly. She wouldn't recognize him with his glasses and hat. He wanted to get outside and be ready when they came out. He'd find out what they were up to. One way or another.

Thirty-six

Kendall thought about Bobbie's plan as she drove up Hamburg turnpike. So engrossed, she never noticed the dark sedan trailing her. Could they pull it off? Did she want to pull it off?

She hit the Ratzer Road 7-Eleven for another diet Dr. Pepper, and then continued on her way.

The medical examiner's office was off Central Ave. in Wayne. It sat deep with the hospital complex, in a red brick building. She felt full from lunch and deep conversation.

As she parked the Firebird in a visitor's spot, her stomach lurched when she spotted a state police cruiser a few cars down gleaming in the sunlight. Please don't let that be who I think it is, she mused.

She pulled open the door and entered a brightly decorated lobby. A place where those waiting could block out the gruesome details that went on inside. She walked up to the receptionist giving her name and signing in. The name before hers was Trooper A. Monroe. Not Mike. Thank goodness.

She sat down and picked up a magazine. She was too nervous to read and merely skimmed the pages until the receptionist called her to go in.

Dr. Bob Crosby met her at the door. "So good to see you Kendall." He hugged her quickly. "I couldn't believe it when you called." He held open a door. "Come on, follow me."

Kendall walked briskly beside him. "You look as handsome as ever Crosby. So who's the lucky lady in your life this week?"

Feigning shock he stopped short. "Oh yeah, by the way, you'll be my assistant today."

She made a face. "Whaaaat?"

"Yup, the state police requested no unauthorized persons attend this autopsy."

"Mike!"

"Who?"

"Oh never mind. Get back to the I'm going to be assisting part. I've never even been to an autopsy before, much less participated." She shook her head. "No way I have to actually cut anything. Right?"

"Only if you want to stay in the room and be part of the autopsy."

"Oh geez." She stomped her foot. "What have I gotten myself into? I hope I don't barf or hit the floor."

His eyebrow rose quickly. "For God's sake, you're a paramedic."

"But it's different when you're trying to save a live person or actively working a cardiac arrest."

"See that door down on the right." He pointed.

She nodded.

"Go in there and put on a pair of blue scrubs, booties, and a hair net."

"You're loving this Crosby, aren't you?" She elbowed him in the ribs.

"Yo, hands off the merchandise sister." He batted her arm away and laughed. "You bet I'm gonna love every minute of this." He strolled away. "Meet you in the autopsy suite, assistant Kendall. It's just through those big, brown doors straight ahead."

She looked through the window running the length of the suite. A short, redheaded state trooper stood stiffly against the wall. "So that's Trooper Monroe, huh?" She pushed open the door. "Hope he's never seen an autopsy before cause this one's gonna be a doozy."

"Beautiful, just beautiful. Blue is definitely your color," said Dr. Crosby as Kendall entered the room fully gowned. "Shall we begin, assistant?"

She wanted to kill him! Edging over to the table she stood beside Crosby. The slightly green-tinged trooper glanced her way and nodded. She nodded back. "Give me a hint here Cros," she whispered.

"Carpenter's in number two." He pointed to the row of body-sized refrigerator units.

Standing next to him, she waited. He elbowed her toward the silver units.

"She's not getting over here by herself."

Kendall shot him a look. Number two was second in from the left, top row. Now how the heck was she going to get the body from there to the exam table? A rolling stretcher hit the back of her legs. "Hey!"

"Just thought I'd help," said Crosby.

The trooper tapped the floor with the tip of his boot. "Ah would you like some help ma'am?" He shot Crosby a disgusted, somewhat greener look.

"Yes, thank you trooper. The good doctor seems too weak to assist me today."

Together they hoisted the body out of the unit onto the gurney and wheeled it over to the table. A striker saw used for cutting the skull sat on the counter behind the right side of the exam table.

"OK troop, the head goes on this side." The body landed with a thud, settling on the metal table set with drains for blood and body fluids.

Kendall sighed with relief and stepped back from the table. Crosby just stood there. Now what's he waiting for? Raising her shoulders with a question, she walked over to the body and picked up the striker saw.

Dr. Crosby jumped between her and the body holding up his hands. "Assistant Kendall you certainly are eager today. I was thinking we would start by examining the entire body for trauma, needle marks. You know anything out of the usual."

Beads of sweat had broken out on the good doctor's forehead. He pointed to the cabinets. "Why don't you set up the syringe and vials for draining the bladder? The label maker is still out of commission, so you'll have to write the victim's name on the urine samples."

If a smile could be sarcastic, hers was. The trooper's skin now had a yellow tinge to go with the green. If this one is still standing by the end of the autopsy, she'd eat his shiny, blue hat. Heck, she might just join him on the floor if things keep going the way they are.

Dr. Crosby pushed the foot pedal to initiate the tape recording of his autopsy findings. Everything he said would be on record.

Kendall fingered her own pocket. A back up to review never hurt. She labeled the containers and set them on the table next to the doctor. Time for making her sweat was over. Nothing could screw up the results.

The autopsy moved slowly, systematically. Things Kendall had not noticed at the scene popped out under the bright lights. The weighing and measuring of the body had been done last night by the evening staff, as had the x-rays and photographs of the body, both dressed and nude. The victims blue teddy had been brown bagged and labeled.

Dr. Crosby began. "Passaic County case 02-6034. The body is that of a twenty-two-year-old American Indian female. She weighs one hundred and ten pounds and is five foot five. The hair is black and eyes dark brown. There are no visible scars or moles. There is a small tattoo on the right hip of a dream catcher symbol. The victim appears to have been in good health. Dental records confirm the body is that of Cheona Carpenter."

Systematically he started his head-to-toe external exam. "On the upper left chest there is a contusion located mid-clavicular to the shoulder." Pressing a ruler to the skin, he angled it over the bruise. "It is eight centimeters wide and appears fairly deep."

Crosby picked up the victims arm closest to him. "There is still mild rigor in the victim's extremities. I note a circumferential mark around the left wrist." He pressed the ruler to the site. "It measures 3/4 inch wide and appears consistent with some type of restraint device. Possibly nylon rope." Gently, he scraped the area to remove debris for microscopic identification.

He proceeded to examine each extremity. "The same type ligature marks are noted on the other wrist and both ankles. Dried blood is noted on the left ankle." He scraped a sample of the dried blood.

Thoroughly, he visually dissected the body. "I find a single tract mark in the right antecubital space with marked bruising in the area of the injection." Lifting up the arm, he checked the back. "Bruising consistent with a hand and fingers noted on the posterior biceps."

Shaking his head, he looked at Kendall and clicked off the mike. "You were right on. So far, nothing is consistent with a drug-induced suicide." He turned the recording on moving down to the genitals. "Vaginal lips appear red. Dried whitish discharge extends from the vaginal opening to the anus."

He took out a swab and inserted it into the canal. "Samples taken to determine if the victim had sexual intercourse before her death." He nodded to the vials Kendall had labeled. "Give me the long one for this swab." Deftly he slid it in then sealed the top. "Please draw the urine sample."

Panic flashed across her face.

Crosby held up his hand. "Sorry. Give me the syringe and I'll do it." Together they worked as a team collecting urine, blood, and body fluids for later analysis.

"OK, ready to make the first cut. Scalpel please."

Moving back up the entire body he made a last cursory exam before cutting. She held out a gleaming silver scalpel. Grasping it, he leaned over the body and cut a y incision, running down from each shoulder, across the breast and meeting in the xiphoid area. From there, he continued cutting a straight line through the abdomen ending at the pubis.

Kendall's stomach growled. She felt herself swaying until she glanced at the trooper. His complexion was now a pale gray-green. "Hey troop. You OK?"

The trooper shook his head no. Grimacing, he swallowed deeply.

"Oh no!" Grabbing his arm she herded him to the sink.

The first hurl came seconds later landing nicely in the steel sink. Several more followed. Kendall patted his back. Behind them a saw buzzed, cutting through Carpenter's ribs and cartilage.

"Kendall, I need you over here please," Crosby called. "He held out the victim's heart."

Regaining her composure, she walked to his side, gagging softly, as he dropped the organ onto her thick blue latex gloves. He pointed to a scale. Blanch white, she carried it to the steel tray and plopped it down.

"On the log next to the scale, write down the weight of every organ I hand you," said the doctor. He held out the lungs.

Nausea rolled into her throat. Get it together Kendall. "Sure no problem Bob." She lifted up the heart.

"What should I do with this?"

"Put it in one of the containers next to the scale."

Methodically she weighed the heart, lungs, esophagus, and trachea.

Once the chest was empty, Crosby peeled back the flaps to the abdomen, revealing yellow globules of fat. "We'll do the same with the organs here. Quickly he cut out the liver, kidneys, spleen, stomach, intestines, and adrenals.

Kendall weighed and recorded, then put each in a separate container for closer exam by Crosby.

"Please take the syringe and draw out the urine from this." He handed her the bladder. "Put the urine in the specimen containers. Blood will tell us for sure, but I always do a quick urine pregnancy test before I remove the female organs. You'll find the box in the cabinet above the sink."

The sink still stunk from the troopers vomit. He requested a few moments outside and hadn't come back in since. She didn't blame him.

Opening the box, she pulled out a pregnancy stick, labeling it with Carpenter's name. Using a dropper she drew urine up then put it on the test strip. This she knew how to do. Thanks to the close call with Mike. It would only take a minute or so to tell if Cheona was pregnant at the time of death. If this turned out to be a murder, then there would be two victims.

Turning back to her workstation, she let the test cook. She watched quietly as Crosby pulled out a pouch-like organ. "What's that Bob?"

"The uterus," he said. "Looks bigger than it should for a non-pregnant female. How's the urine test coming?"

Picking up the white tube she gasped. "Shit, it's positive."

"I was afraid of that," he said. "It appears we have two victims here. "Give me that container," he said pointing to a round dish. "I'll have to send out all the swabs and the fetus for DNA testing now."

Quickly, she set the pregnancy stick on the top shelf. Handing the specimen container to Crosby, she asked, "How far along was she?"

"That will be for the FBI forensic lab to determine." Opening a drawer, he pulled out a speculum using it to open the vagina. Examine it for tears, bruising, anything suggestive of a violent attack.

"Nothing unusual about the vaginal exam. Findings do suggest the victim possibly had intercourse shortly before she died. Force does not seem to be a factor at this time."

Silent tears fell for the precious life that had been taken before it began. "How could someone do this?"

Bob shut down the recorder. "You'd make one smart detective Kendall. If you messed up at the scene, none of this would have come out. Heck I doubt we'd be doing an autopsy on an OD."

"So you think foul play is involved here too?"

He shook his head yes. "This isn't a simple overdose. That much I can tell you." He handed her the ovaries. "We'll know more once we get back the tox. and DNA reports."

"CJ and I won't stop until the truth is out. I haven't felt this strongly about anything in a long time Bob. My parents' deaths really knocked the wind out of my sails, but I feel a breeze picking up."

"You're a good egg," Crosby said, with a sad smile.

"You know Bob, I think I'm getting the hang of this job."

The striker saw buzzed to life shattering the silence of the room. "What are you doing with that?" she shouted.

While she had been talking, the doctor had made an incision at the top of the skull running from ear to ear.

"Come here and pull the scalp down over the face."

"No way," she said. Shaking, she backed away from the table. "I...I just can't do it."

Setting down the saw, he made a face. "You are sure you're a paramedic right?" He grasped the flesh and slowly pulled the skin up and away revealing the white bone of the skull. "The last things I have to do are cut the skull and take out the brain."

"Oh gosh, the brain." She wiped the sweat off her forehead with the back of her gown. "Do I have to stay?"

"Yes!" He stomped his foot soundly. "I'm risking my job for you to be here today. So you damn well better help me."

"I'll do the best I can," she mumbled inching toward him. "Wha...a..t do you want me to do?"

"First, put your face shield on and make sure no skin is exposed."

Pulling down the plastic face shield, she stood ready. Ready to pass out if he really cut into the skull. Tell her this wasn't happening.

The saw charged back to life. Watery bone fragments flew onto her scrubs and face shield. Please let this be over soon. she prayed. Mercifully the saw shut down a few minutes later and Crosby began to remove the brain.

The autopsy was longer and more tedious than she had expected. Each organ that had been weighed had then been sectioned and dissected for examination. The last one would be the brain. Once they were finished, all the organs would be bagged and stuffed back into the body for burial. Except in Chenoa's case, her uterus with the fetus inside would be sent out to the crime lab for further testing.

Scooping the organs up, she placed them together in a plastic bag. Crosby finished his exam of the brain.

"No evidence of hemorrhage or trauma to the head, brain, or neck." Pausing for a moment in thought he continued. "Based on the evidence noted so far, the estimated time of death is between three a.m. and 4:30 a.m. The cause of death was massive injection of heroin causing respiratory and cardiac arrest. As of this point in time, the manner of death is being classified a homicide."

He clicked off the mike just as the trooper walked back into the room. "Sorry," was all he could muster. His face matched the color of his hair. "I guess I'd better turn down autopsy details in the future."

Kendall smiled. "Just takes a little getting used to."

Crosby cocked his head and coughed.

"Well it does!" Kendall said smartly.

Crosby rolled his eyes and walked over to the bag of organs. Carefully, he stuffed the remains back into the body cavity.

Kendall looked at the girl so beautiful in life lying on a stainless steel table, gutted from end to end like a deer. Nausea and churning resumed inside her sour stomach. "Ah, need anything else Dr. Crosby?"

He glanced about the sparkling clean autopsy suite. "Not bad for a newbie. Of course women are good for cleaning."

Hands on hips, she swaggered over with a snappy retort, freezing in her steps as Crosby squished the brain back into the gaping head and corked it with the skull.

She heard him giggling softly to himself. The sink was only two feet away, the yellow tinged trooper three, and the door five. Racing for the door she ripped it open and ran down the hall to the locker room.

Thirty-seven

Stupid bitch! She hadn't even noticed him as she raced past him down the hall. What had been bluer, her face or scrubs, he couldn't decide. He snarled menacingly. How the hell did she get herself into the fucking autopsy? What had they found out? What!

Did they know yet that the bitch had been pregnant with a bastard she'd tried to say was his? He always used condoms. Cheona had laughed at him and held up a sewing needle. The conniving bitch. She wanted him to marry her. To give her and the baby his name. No way was he going to soil his name with some money-hungry cunt and her little bastard. He knew she'd slept with other men. Several.

Still, if they knew and it came back positive for his DNA he'd face murder one. It was now 4:45 p.m.. Crosby always left at five no matter what he had cooking. Swiftly, he walked to an unused lab and locked himself inside. He could stick around until the place closed. The skeleton crew on duty wouldn't even know he was here. But Cheona would. Won't you darling, he spat.

Peeking out the darkened window he watched Crosby carry the autopsy file into his office. The trooper followed, shooting out questions, but Crosby pointed to his watch. With a toss, the file landed on the desk in the chief medical examiner's office. Crosby said something he couldn't hear to his secretary, and then pulled the door shut smiling at Kendall dragging herself down the hall.
"Cros," he heard her say. "I won't do your job for all the dough in the world."

He merely patted her arm. "Funny that's exactly how I feel about yours. See, my patients never give me an attitude or talk back."

Starting down the hall, Kendall rolled her eyes. "Come on, I've had enough."

"I should be able to finish up tomorrow. Everything is secured in the lock up freezer. Nobody could get into that if they tried."

"You sure?" asked the trooper.

"Yes." He held out his arm. "I assure you what happened today is perfectly normal for a first autopsy." He winked conspiratorially. "I'll never tell, will you Kendall?"

"My lips are sealed. What Mike doesn't know won't hurt him."

The voices slowly disappeared down the hall. "Mike Garcia..," he heard the trooper say.

He'd wait a half hour or so, and then get to work. Stupid moron. Nobody huh. Well meet Mr. Nobody. I'm going to screw up your little autopsy so much, you won't know what hit you. He settled down to wait."

Thirty-eight

Lt. Grey was waiting for her when she got home at 6:30. He got out of his marked cruiser and met her as she was getting out of the Firebird. "Hello Paramedic Rose." Flipping open a note pad he continued, "I have a few more follow-up questions for you."

She stared back at him with a scowl. "How did you know what time I would be home?"

Grey didn't smile. "I didn't."

"So you sat here all day waiting?"

"Actually I asked your downstairs neighbor ah..," he glanced at his pad.,"Mr. Park. He said if you were working you'd be home around eight. It's such a beautiful area." He gestured with his hands. "I figured I'd catch up on some paperwork and enjoy the scenery."

This guy had a chip on his shoulder and she didn't know why. "Would you like to come in? It's pretty damp out here." She walked to her door. "Coming?" she said when he made no move.

"Ah, yeah, sure," he stuttered.

"You're acting like I'm the suspect or something," she said pausing at the top of the stairs. She twisted the knob. Below, her neighbor's door opened.
"Is everything alright Kendall?" asked Tom Park.

"I'm not sure Tom. Lt. Grey here seems to be eyeing me suspiciously. I think he's afraid to be alone with me." She flashed a quick smile at the young cop.

Grey appeared shocked. "That's not it at all Ms. Rose." He stumbled on the steps. Grasping the railing, he hoisted himself back up, red face and all. "First day with my new feet," he said humorously.

"So you're not the tough sour puss after all." Walking into the kitchen she set down her purse on the counter and called, "I'll be fine Tom. Thanks."

Grey followed meekly. "Garrison's still in critical condition." Grey motioned toward a chair. "Mind if I sit down? It's been a long night and day."

Kendall saw the weariness in his hazel eyes. "Have you been to bed since last night?"

"If you call two hours on the station sofa, then yes." He sighed. "I'm sorry I came off like a hard ass. There are just a lot of unanswered questions about what happened here last night."

"How about a hot cup of tea?"

"That would be wonderful. I wish this nasty weather would break." Removing his navy uniform jacket he set it over the back of the kitchen chair. "Janice Garrison and her son's Billy and Jack don't seem real sorry Garrison's lying in ICU."

"I wonder which one of his sons he implicated last night?"

"Implicated?" He looked back at her quizzically.

Kendall hesitated. "Ah yes. With all the excitement Officer Black forgot to tell you Garrison said something about his son before he collapsed."

Grey raised his eyebrows. "Forgot or omitted?" He took the steaming tea she handed him and sipped it, then set it down with a thud. "Look!" he said sharply. "I need to know what's going on here. No more beating around the bush!"

"You aren't the only one Lt. Grey. I assure you," she said calmly. "Let me start from the beginning and then you'll see what we've been dealing." She took a sip of tea and began. "Yesterday, in the capacity of a paramedic, I was called to do a pronouncement..."

Thirty-nine

Johnnie's cell phone rang at nineteen twenty hours. He glanced at the caller ID and answered in a hushed voice. "Hello Kendall."

"Johnnie Black?" said a male voice.

"Yes, who is this?" He inched into a room and shut the door.

"Lt. Grey from Warwick police. I have a few questions about last night,"

"Where is Kendall?"

"She's right here. She's told me everything,"

"What?" he spat into the phone. "Why don't you stop fucking with me and tell me what it is you want Grey,"

"Such language. How unbecoming of an officer," he snapped back.

"Sorry. I'm under a bit of pressure at the moment. I really don't have time to talk. Would it be possible to meet you later?"

"I don't see any harm in that. One question before you hang up. Did you have to use force to subdue Garrison?" In the back ground a door slammed. "Hello Black. Are you still there?"

The line went dead.

Andy Grey hung up the phone.

"Well what did he say?" asked Kendall.

"Said he was busy and he'd get back to me later. This guy is a little high strung, huh?" He looked at Kendall sympathetically.

"I don't know about that," she replied, setting the phone back on the counter. "I just met him yesterday at the pronouncement."

Grey looked back speculatively. "You two seemed awfully cozy last night."

"I was a bit shaken." She sipped her tea. "He's been nothing but nice and respectful to me. Could it be your testosterone levels both peaked at the same time?"

Surprise registered on his face. "Ah, a girl with a bit of humor. A small bit." Stretching his arms he yawned. "So you aren't involved with him?"

"Not yet." She rubbed her neck. "But I'm thinking about it."

A knock sounded from the outer door. "Must be CJ."

Grey grabbed her wrist. "I know I don't have any right to say this, but be careful about Black. People aren't always what they appear to be."

She nodded. "Don't I know it." Glancing down at his left hand. "Married Lt. Grey?"

He let go of her wrist with a start. "Ah, no."

Tom was at the door with CJ. "Hey girlfriend, come on in and join the party."

CJ looked at Tom.

"I know nothing," he said with a German accent. "Nothing at all."

"Thanks for getting the door Tom. Hey, want to join us for dinner?"

"Are you cooking?" he said, glancing at his watch. "Cause I can still make it to CVS for some Pepto-Bismol."

"Aaaa haaa haaa." Kendall shot him a look.

"I'm on Tom's side," said CJ.

Kendall heard laughing behind her. "No help from you either, Officer Grey." Holding her head high she said, "Since no one appreciates a true artist in their own life time, we will be going to the China Queen buffet."

Applause sounded from the stairs. Bela woofed. "I feel so under appreciated sometimes," Kendall said sourly. Maxie jumped up onto the table. "Meow."

"Even my own kids are turning against me." Picking up Max she petted his soft fur, then plopped him onto the floor. "Enough of that young man."

Grey stood up and put on his jacket. "I guess I best be going. My shift ended two hours ago."

"Why don't you join us then?" said Kendall brightly.

Tom and CJ walked in the kitchen. Andy Grey took one look at CJ and blushed. "I don't want to impose."

"Come on Grey. Our treat." Kendall slapped him on the back. "You can tell me more of your gut feeling about Johnnie Black."

"Well, OK. I just need to return the car and I'll meet you there." He smiled at CJ, "Say around eight-fifteen?"

CJ blushed back. "Sounds good," she said softly.

Kendall and Tom shot each other amusing looks as they followed CJ and Andy outside.

"Tom, you driving?" said Kendall.

"What's the matter the old tub leaking again?" He pointed at the Firebird.

"Take that back Park!" She lunged at him. "She's a classic."

Evading her he ran to the driver's side and yanked open the door of his 2000 green Ford Explorer.

She poked him with her finger. "Take it back."

"OK, OK!" Laughing he rolled onto the seat. "You win. She's a classic."

Andy looked at CJ. "Are they always like this?"

CJ's shoulders shook with a giggle. "When it comes to that car, all I've got to say is watch out." She patted the rusty, blue metal. "In 1979 I was only eight years old. She's a classic all right."

"Let's see," said Grey. "In 1979 I was nine." He looked her over appraisingly. "I'm only a year older than you, huh."

"Come on you two. Cut the googly eyes and let's go. I'm starving," yelled Kendall.

Simultaneous blushing ensued. "See you there," said CJ.

"I'm looking forward to it," said Grey.

Forty

Things had gone exceptionally well. He held up his gloved hands. "With these, I have erased every trace of me." He covered his mouth to stifle a high-pitched laugh.

Merrily, he trotted over to the chief medical examiner's secure computer. Now to place my little warning to Crosby on his e-mail.

Wouldn't mommy be proud of her little boy? He hugged himself. He needed mommy. She'd make everything better. Sweat broke out over his body. His cock grew hard against his will. No! No! He could feel her hands wrap around his dick pulling it to her dripping hole. Shoving it inside, she'd smack his bare ass with a spoon until he thrust into her.

He slid to the floor. I was only ten damn you. Tears dripped onto his scrubs. I wanted to play with kids my age not your big swaying tits. She'd turned him into what he was today.

Someday real soon, mommy would be the one stuffed into the ice-cold freezer. Someday he'd cut those pendulous globs of fat right off her chest and stuff them up her smelly hole. He hit the on switch and hacked into the private files of Dr. Bob Crosby and began to type.

Forty-one

Life was good for Dr. Bob Crosby. He loved his job and the status it brought him, not to mention the money. He walked up the steps to his Franklin Lakes mansion, opening the door, and shutting off the alarm. He never dreamed he would live in a place as cool as this.

From his Frigidaire with automatic ice and water, he poured himself a glass of white zinfandel, and then walked to his home office. He planned to check his e-mail, watch a little TV, drink a little more wine, and then hit the hay in his new king-size water bed.

Setting the glass on a coaster, he reached down and turned on the computer. Running his hands over the expensive cherry desk, he thought back on the case he started today. He really should have finished up the paperwork before he left. Oh well, it could wait until morning. The girl hadn't killed herself with heroin. He didn't know what had happened, but he sure as hell was going to find out. He wasn't the chief medical examiner for nothing.

Sitting on his new, plush maroon chair, he typed his online password. He loved coming home to messages. In the left corner an instant message blinked.

Somebody's on line right now talking to me. Whoever was logged on had a similar password to his at work. ME1 flashed at him, making him look twice. The only computer he used that on was the one at the medical examiner's office.

He grabbed the keyboard, freezing as he read the message. Someone was in his office right now. 'Dear little girl lover,' it began. How could anyone know about that?

His parents had it erased from his records. It had been a mistake; he hadn't known what he was doing.

Sweat beads broke out on his forehead. NO! This can't be happening. Whoever was in his office, was threatening to ruin his life and career. Dear God no. What did the guy want?

He logged on. "Who are you?"

"Wouldn't you like to know big man?"

"Stop it. You don't know anything."

"Don't I? How's your little friend Sally doing?"

"Shut up! Shut up! You friggin' freak. Why are you doing this?"

The screen remained blank with no reply.

"Are you still there ME1?"

"I left you a little present."

"Where?"

"Where do you think moron?"

"You can't tell anyone what you know!"

"Oh can't I? Just watch, you sick bastard,"

"Why are you doing this?"

"We really must get together real soon."

ME1 signed off before he could reply. What the hell was going on? Hanging his head, he began to cry. Tears fell over his beautiful cherry desk. Should he call the police? No. Then they'd find out. He'd be ruined. Nothing was going to wreck his success. Nothing!

He picked up his keys and jacket and left. If the guy is still there, he'll kill him. Surprising a burglar at work would be classified self-defense, for sure.

He sped out of his development not bothering to turn on the wipers as a heavy mist began to fall.

Forty-two

Garcia looked at the clock. April second, twenty-one-hundred on the dot.

Dialing Kendall's cell phone, he lay back in the swivel desk chair. On the fourth ring she answered. Loud voices hovered in the background as she said hello.

"Hi, Kendall. It's Mike."

"Still mad at me Mike?"

"No." He sat up straight. "I wasn't mad at you. I came up there hoping to work things out between us. When I saw Black, I guess I lost it." He rubbed his temple.

"Should have stuck around for the show."

"Excuse me?" he said.

"The Garrison-shoves-his-way-in-and-attacks-me show. Thank God for Johnnie. If he hadn't been there I don't think I'd be talking to you now."

"Shit Kendall. Why didn't you call me?"

Holding her finger to her lips she motioned the group to be quiet. "Actually, I'm having dinner with the investigating officer from Warwick PD."

"Figures," he mumbled.

"Here, let me put him on." She handed Grey the phone. "It's Mike Garcia, the trooper in charge of the Willow Run investigation. Would you tell him about last night?"

"Ah, sure." Grabbing the phone he introduced himself and filled Mike in on the incident.

Kendall waved to CJ. "How about we go to the ladies' room?"

"I don't have to go," said CJ.

Kendall craned her head toward Andy Grey and coughed.

"Oh. Yes, the ladies' room."

"Hurry back soon gab-a-gals," said Tom.

Minutes later Kendall cornered CJ. "So do you like him?"

CJ blushed.

'Since when do you get tongue tied?"

"Since tonight." At the mirror, CJ combed through her hair with her fingers. "He's so cute." She turned to Kendall. "Do you think he likes me?"

"Ah, duh." Kendall lifted the lip-gloss wand gleaming with light apricot color and applied it to her pouting mouth. "If he turns any redder when he's around you, I'm taking his temp and checking for heat stroke."

CJ appraised herself in the mirror. "I haven't been on a date in so long."

"Well get ready sister, cause if I have anything to do with it you'll be going out real soon."

Noses powdered and gossip shared, they walked back to the table. Grey was still engrossed in conversation. Tom was staring at a sexy guy waiting for takeout.

"What happened to your boyfriend, Rich?" said Kendall.

Tom smiled. "You know what they say. 'When you stop looking you're dead.'"

"Men!" said CJ.

"Can't live with 'em. Can't leave 'em on the side of the road 'cause they always find their way back home," said Kendall.

Grey handed the phone back to Kendall with a look of amusement on his face. "Speaking of men, this one wants to speak with you again."

"Can I come by tonight when I get off work?" asked Mike.

"Its nine-fifteen already. I'm worn out from last night," said Kendall.

"I'll leave now and be there by ten. Please Kendall. I really need to see you."

She softened. "Ten is fine. See you then." She pushed off, disconnecting before Mike could say anything else.

"Shall we," said Tom.

CJ reached for the check.

"Oh no you don't; this one's on me," said Andy.

CJ blushed releasing the paper. "Thanks Lt. Grey."

Andy smiled. "I think we can be a little less formal now that we've shared sum yung cat, don't you?" Grey said in a bad Chinese accent.

CJ turned redder. "OK. Thanks Andy."

In unison, Kendall and Tom said overly sweet. "Thanks Lt. Grey!"

Andy looked shyly away.

"Say Tom, I need something at the grocery store." She turned to Grey. "Andy would you mind dropping CJ back at my place? She has a long ride home and I don't want to drag her all over creation?"

Andy brightened. "I'd be happy to." He opened the door. "OK with you CJ?"

"More than OK," she answered, winking at Kendall.

They said their goodbyes in the parking lot, dashing between the raindrops to their cars, and headed off in separate directions.

Forty-three

CJ and Andy were gone by the time they got home. Tom parked the Explorer and helped her carry the order upstairs. "Need help putting this stuff away?"

Kendall glanced at her pager checking the time. "No thanks. Mike's due any minute. I'll put him to work."

"If you need me I'm right downstairs." He paused at the door. A serious look covered his face. "Kendall, be careful. Don't get hurt." He left closing the door behind him.

She set the last bag on the kitchen table. "I'll put away all the frozen stuff first in case Mike shows up early."

At five past ten she saw car lights shining through the rain from her bow window in the kitchen. "Bela, want to go out?"

The dog raced to the door, pawing at the floor.

Kendall opened it and the yellow dog ran down the stairs. At the bottom she turned around with a look in her eyes that could only say, 'Come on mom!'

Grabbing her rain jacket, she took the steps two at a time, reaching the door at the same time Mike did. As she flung it open Bela ran down the step hurling herself at all two hundred and two pound of Mike.

"Yikes!" he cried.

She laughed heartily. "Come on now Mike, you out weigh her by a hundred and two pounds!"

"Watch it missy. I outweigh you by about that much too. He handed her a bunch of wildflowers. "These are for you."

She inhaled deeply. "They are beautiful. Thank you so much." She carried them inside. "Come in out of the rain." Inside the doorway she watched Bela sniffing the ground. "Come on girl. Want a treat?"

Bela ran inside, up the stairs, skidding to a stop in front of her cabinet. "Woof."

"Easy now," said Mike. He walked to the cabinet and knelt next to Bela. "What would you like?"

"Woof! Huff!"

He took out two treats and set them on the ground. "Wait," he said, holding up his hand.

Bela sat staring at the treats.

"OK!" Mike gave the release.

Bela leaped on the treats gobbling them up. Wagging her stumpy tail she eyeballed Mike.

"That's it girl. Go get your bone."

Kendall watched the interaction. "Kind of easy to fall back into the old ways."

Mike looked up at her. "It sure is." He had a sappy look on his face as he stood up and came to her. "I've missed you Kendall. More than you know."

Her gaze didn't waiver from his. "I've missed you too."

"But?"

"Yes there always is that but. But I can't forget what happened. You hurt me more than you'll ever know."

"I was scared."

"How do you think I felt?"

"Scared?"

"Scared, pregnant, and abandoned."

"I am so sorry."

"Then you dragged CJ into it. Mike, how could you do that?" Sudden cold coursed through her. "You knew she had a crush on you." Anger welled up, dredging up feelings she had tried so hard to bury.

Mike faced her, tenderly taking her cold hands into his. "Liquor can make a man do things he won't do sober. That's not an excuse. I guess it is more of an explanation. I was hurt, angry, deflated when I showed up at CJ's". Raising her hands he kissed each one lightly. "I needed comfort."

Kendall looked away. "Comfort in the arms of my best friend. That's the ultimate betrayal."

He nodded. "You're right. I was an asshole. There are no excuses in the world that could make what we did right." Encircling his arms around her back he held her to his broad chest.

"I ruined something I had dreamed about all my life. I've never loved anyone like I have you. We clicked from the moment we met and our relationship only got better. I wanted to spend the rest of my life with you."

She nestled her head on his chest. "I only needed time Mike. Time to put my fears to rest and realize that life with you was the best thing I'd ever be offered."

She wiped away a tear. "I was so excited driving to your house. I had the pregnancy test and a ring."

"A ring?"

She moved from his arms. "I've kept it all this time. I don't know why, but I just couldn't get rid of it."

Mike followed her down the hall, to the bedroom closet. Standing on her tippy toes she reached for a metal box on the top shelf.

"Here let me get that," he said nervously.

From the shelf he lifted down a fire safe box, setting it on the bed. Kendall opened it with a key and removed a small velvet box. She handed the box to him. "Go ahead open it."

With trembling hands he lifted the lid. Inside was a silver band set with small diamonds. Tears threatened to roll from his eyes. "It's beautiful."

"Read the inscription inside," said Kendall. Lifting out the ring she handed it to him.

"To Mike, the man who opened my eyes to what real love is. Yes!" The tears won't stop now. He grabbed Kendall crushing her to his body. He slipped the ring on his left hand. "Please tell me I can make this right." His voice cracked with emotion. "My life has been miserable and lonely as hell without you."

Looking at him sadly she said, "It would take a lot of time to rebuild my trust Mike."

Reaching up she stroked his brown hair. "I'm not ready to jump back into a serious relationship with you." His tears dampened her face.

"I've got all the time in the world." He pulled back. Looking in her eyes he said, "I love you. I've never stopped loving you. Whatever it takes to get us back together I'll do it."

"What about Johnnie Black?"

"What about him?" Mike asked sharply. "If you want to keep seeing him, I have no right to stop you. I won't be happy about it. Whatever it takes to get back to where we were I'll do it." He kissed her lips, softly at first then more demanding. "Baby I love you," he whispered.

"So many lonely nights I've missed you," she whispered breathlessly in his ear.

Hungrily she kissed his neck, inhaling the scent of obsession. "Make love to me Mike."

Pushing her away he searched her face. "Are you sure Kendall?"

Traveling her hands down his back, she locked eyes with him and slid her hands over the rough texture of his jeans cupping him. "Yes."

Muscles tensed as his powerful body came to life. Kneeling before her, he slowly lowered the zipper to her jeans.

"Um," she murmured. Grasping the waist, tantalizingly slow, he pulled them down her body until they lay crumbled on the floor.

Burying his face into her pink panties, he licked the silky material with his tongue. He pleaded, "Let me taste you."

Her legs started shaking and she had to brace her hands on his shoulders. "It's been so long Mike." Parting her legs she leaned back.

He held her with his strong hands grasping her butt. Grasping the panties with his teeth he pulled them down exposing her. With one hand he supported her then slowly slid his fingers inside her.

"Does that feel good love?" He jerked his finger in and out of her.

"I want you inside me," she murmured greedily.

He started to release her. She pushed him back. "Remember my favorite position?"

Smiling, he grabbed her hips elevating her above him as he lay down on his back. "I remember very well."

Like a schoolboy he fumbled with his zipper until he released his manhood—red, engorged, hard. Wrapping his hand around it he held it straight. "Slide on my love."

Moaning softly, she lowered herself onto his legs. "I have to get a condom baby."

Reaching across him she opened the nightstand drawer and pulled out a box. Ripping open a green packet she straddled him again. Leaning forward, nibbling on his lip, she grasped his member, slowly unrolling the latex onto him.

Teasing, hovering above his hard shaft, she slowly impaled herself. "Why am I the only one who's naked here?"

She grabbed his shirt, rocking back and pulled it over his head. "That's better."

She inhaled deeply taking in the sight of his rock hard chest. Lying prone she moved quickly, rubbing on his body, moaning loudly with each thrust.

He matched her thrust, watching pleasure envelope her features. "Come sweetheart," he moaned.

When she was sated he thrust deeply coming with a groan. "I'll last longer next time. Promise," he said.

Rolling off him she lay on her side molding to his body. "Um that was so good," she whispered. Stroking his inner thigh, she asked, "Ready for round two?"

Mike inhaled sharply. "You always were insatiable." Reaching out he cupped her breast teasing the nipple with his fingers.

Encircling him she said. "I see you don't have a problem rising to the occasion." Lowering her mouth she tasted every inch of him.

When he was ready to come he rolled on top of her teasing her. Slowly he slid a condom on.

"Please Mike. I can't take it much longer." Grasping his buttock she jerked down pushing him inside her. "That's better."

"Quite the hussy Ms. Rose," he said playfully.

"You know me Mike. When I see something I want, I take it."

Moving together like a well-oiled machine he waited until she came, locking eyes with her he moaned, "I love you Kendall."

On the bedside table his cell phone rang, breaking the spell. Regrettably he rolled off her. "Sorry honey I have to take this. I'm on call." He answered the phone; it was 23:05 by his watch.

Jumping from the bed, picking up his scattered clothes, he said. "I have to leave. There's been a break in at the medical examiner's. Get dressed, I think you'll want to come. Crosby's been taken to Saint Joe's with a bullet wound to the head."

Forty-four

The uniform at the door waved Mike through. He held out his hand stopping Kendall. "Only police," he said.

"She's with me," said Mike.

The uniform nodded, allowing her pass.

They walked quickly down the hall, past the locker rooms to the chief medical examiner's suite. A trooper guarded the door. "Just need to see some identification sir."

Garcia flashed him his badge. "Paramedic Rose," he said introducing Kendall to the trooper.

"Ah, OK," said the trooper. He let her pass following Garcia into the inner office.

Kendall gasped at the scene before her. Blood splatter covered the wall behind Crosby's desk. On the floor lay a bloody endotracheal tube, trauma dressings, and oxygen mask—all discarded equipment used by the paramedics trying to save his life.

Shock registered on her face when she saw the folder sitting on the desktop was Cheona Carpenter's final autopsy report.

"Mike, look at the file folder." Kendall pointed.

Putting on latex gloves he picked up the file without disturbing any other evidence. "Looks like he was working late."

Kendall shook her head. "Not unless he came back to the office after we left."

"We?" said Mike, surprised. "When did you see Crosby?"

She shuffled her feet. "Today. I assisted him with the autopsy."

"Assisted?" He walked to her and grabbed her arm dragging her out of the office and into the hall. "What are you talking about?"

"I've known Dr. Crosby for a number of years, so I called him and asked to sit in on the Carpenter autopsy."

Mike scowled. "I made it clear to Dr. Crosby that no unauthorized persons were to be present."

"I wasn't unauthorized. His assistant was out today and I filled in." Kendall rubbed her hands together. "Now can we put the fact I was there behind us and take a look at the file."

Mike smiled slightly. "Did you really think I didn't know you were here today?"

She cocked her head. "You did? And you let me stay anyway?"

He nodded. "Yes. When I heard the trooper they sent to secure the autopsy, I figured I needed someone on the inside who would at least stay conscious."

She laughed. "It was touch and go there for a while."

Raising his eyebrows, he looked down into her eyes. "You said Crosby left with you after the autopsy was completed?"

"Yes that's just it. The autopsy paperwork wasn't finished. Plus he'd sent the fetus to the crime lab..."

"Fetus?" interrupted Mike.

"Yes. Cheona Carpenter was pregnant at the time of her death. So if you find a completed file than Bob came back to the office after we all left and finished." She shook her head rapidly. "That doesn't sound like the Bob Crosby I know and love." Her body began to shake.

Mike bowed his head. "He's in surgery at St. Joe's if you want to go down there."

"I really should. Bob hasn't been close to his family in years." She looked up at Mike. "First would you let me check over the file and see if it adds up to what I assisted with today?"

"I really can't do that honey." He patted her arm. "I'm sorry. It's evidence in the investigation."

Squinting her eyes she said, "You could still let me see it. After all I participated in it."

"No!" Mike backed away from her. "You've pushed your way into this investigation up until now." Turning he locked eyes with her. "Let me handle it from here. No more interference from you or CJ." He pointed his finger at her chest. "Get it?"

Kendall shot him a menacing glance. "Oh I get it Mike."

"Kendall this has nothing to do with us or our personal relationship." He took a step toward her.

"Doesn't it Mike?" She stepped back. "Once again you are acting as if I'm no more than a piece of arm candy."

She poked him back in his chest with her finger. "You've never appreciated the fact I actually have a brain." She turned and walked away missing the look that shot across the trooper's handsome face.

"Call me with an update on Crosby's condition," he called.

She waved without turning around. "I'm taking your truck. Find a ride home."

Mike shrugged his shoulders. He opened the manila file and began to read.

Forty-five

The emergency room at St. Joseph's Hospital in Paterson was hopping tonight. Kendall pushed through the double door to the trauma room. The bloody remnants of the resuscitation lay scattered on the floor. Bob, what happened?

She left the room and went in search of the charge nurse Alice. She found her at the nurse's station.

"Hi Kendall," she said glancing up. "What brings you out tonight?"

"Dr. Bob Crosby."

Alice looked up sharply. "You knew him?"

"Knew?" said Kendall, inhaling sharply.
Alice stood up and put her arms around Kendall's shoulder. "Come on, lets go in the break room and talk."

They walked through the crowded ER, down the hall to the nurse's lounge.

"Have a seat," Alice said softly. "Would you like some tea or coffee?"

"Tea would be great. Plain with two sugars, please."

She set the tea on the table and sat down next to Kendall. "How long have you known Crosby?"

"Around nine years." She took a sip of the hot liquid, which did nothing to quell the stark, cold fear building inside her. "I know you're being kind Alice, but tell me the truth."

"Crosby made it through surgery but he's going to be a vegetable."

"Oh no!" cried Kendall. "Not Bob."

Alice handed her a tissue. "I just can't believe he shot himself."

"Shot himself?" said Kendall. "What are you talking about? I worked with him yesterday and he was fine. He had the world by the balls."

"Really?" Alice leaned back in her chair. "Sometimes when we are close to someone we don't see the signs..."

Kendall held up her hand. "I will never believe he killed himself. Never!" She stood up. "Do you think they will let me see him?"

Alice stood up and gave her a hug. "Sure kiddo. I'll call upstairs and let them know you're coming."

"Thanks Alice." She squeezed her hand. "I'll stop down and let you know how he's doing before I leave."

She took the elevators to the second floor. The nurses smiled sadly and pointed to a darkened corner room. One of them got up and met her.

"Kendall, it's not a pretty sight. I just wanted to warn you."

"I understand," said Kendall. She walked into the room gasping at the horrific sight before her. "Are you sure this is Bob?"

The nurse nodded. "We've identified him through finger prints and dental records. It is Dr. Crosby."

"My dear friend. I'm so sorry." Kendall grasped his hand filled with IV lines, running life-sustaining medication into what remained of Bob Crosby. "The gun must have been forced into his mouth. He was so handsome. Did you know him?"

The nurse shook her head with pity, both for Dr. Crosby and for Kendall's denial. "No, I didn't. I understand he was a very nice man."

Kendall thought back to the bloody scene at the medical examiner's office. She didn't have to wonder what had been splattered on the wall behind the desk.

"I loved Bob," she said. "But he was vainer than most women I know. He never would have mutilated his face this way." Gently she touched what remained of his forehead. Hollow sockets once filled with sparkling blue eyes gaped back at her. Nothing remained of his nose and mouth except for a few teeth in the back.

She listened to the whoosh of the ventilator blowing air through the intubation tube. It was the only thing keeping the shell of her friend alive.

"He wouldn't want to be kept like this." Kendall looked at the nurse. "Have you contacted his family yet?"

"We are still trying. Several messages have been left. So far nobody has called back."

Kendall bowed her head. "I'm not surprised. Bob hasn't spoken to his family in years. Something had estranged them. He never could bring himself to tell me what it was."

She squeezed his hand gently. "I'm here with you Bob."

"I have to take care of other patients now," said the nurse sympathetically. "If you need anything call me."

"OK, thank you," said Kendall. "I'll only stay a little while."

"Stay as long as you want honey."

Kendall pulled a chair next to the hospital bed and snaked her hand through the railing. Gently she held his hand and began to reminisce how they first met.

Forty-six

Black dialed her number again, for the fourth time in an hour. Where was she? He paced the floor of the muster room waiting for his relief to show up. He hoped to meet up with her after work.

He glanced at his watch. It read 23:55 and, as usual, his relief was just squeaking in under the wire.

Sgt. McKay entered the room. "So Black how did your detail go?"

Black turned around with a grin. "Real good Sgt. Real good. I even finished up a little early."

McKay slapped him on the back. "My protégé. Want to get a beer after work?"

Black whistled. "Not tonight my man. Tonight I have a date with a beautiful lady."

"Nothing new there. I don't think I've ever seen you with anything less than spectacular. So who's the latest one?"

Johnnie handed him the log sheet with his mileage and tour information. "I think I really like this one Sam."

"Oh yeah?"

"I met her on the overdose call. She's a Wayne General paramedic," said Black. He bent down to unzip his boot. "Looks like my relief showed up at midnight on the dot as usual."

"Good evening to you too, Officer Black," said Ron Hutter. "Sorry I'm not here at a quarter-of like you, but I have a life." He glanced at the call log. "I see you handled all of one call tonight. And you actually wrote one whole ticket at six-fifteen. Wow, that's a record for you. How's your hand? Do you have writer's cramp?" Hutter's menacing laugh filled the squad room.

"Very funny Hutter. Lucky for you, looks aren't everything." Black changed into blue jeans and a white tee shirt.

Pulling on his brown cowboy boots he turned to the Sgt. "Thanks for the invite tonight Sam. Can I take a rain check?"

Sam smiled and slapped him on the back. "Sure, that's no problem." He winked. "Enjoy yourself tonight."

"Oh got another date Black?" said Hutter. "Your hair looks a little dull tonight. What's the matter? Run out of peroxide?"

Black rolled his eyes. "You really are a moron Hutter." He opened the outside door. "See you Sam."

Yanking open the door to his Mercedes he slid in behind the wheel, dialing her cell again.

"Hello," said a strangled voice.

"Kendall, are you all right? What's wrong?"

Sobbing filled the other end. "Bob."

"Bob? Who's Bob? What happened?" Black paused listening to the sorrow on the other end of the line. "Honey, tell me where you are?"

"Saint Joe's emergency," she managed to get out through the sobs.

"Stay there. I'm leaving work right now and I'll be there in less than a half hour."

He hit the gas of the black sports car, burning rubber out of the parking lot. "Hang in there sweetheart. I'm coming."

Forty-seven

Mike picked up the autopsy report from the desk where he'd thrown it. It was all there in black and white. Accidental death by heroin overdose. Crosby's conclusion was clear; there was no foul play involved. He searched the pages again. Nothing!

Tossing the file he leaned back in the chair. He needed to talk to Kendall. Picking up the phone he dialed her cell. Come on sweetie answer. He tapped a pen on the table, the sound echoing in the silent conference room. She picked up on the third ring. He could tell she'd been crying.

"Hello baby. How is he?"

She sobbed softly. "He's a vegetable Mike. He's got tubes, wires, and medications keeping his body alive. But he's not there." He heard her gasp.

"What is it honey?"

"His face is gone. It was blown off in the attack."

"Kendall, calm down." He wasn't sure how to continue. Evidence was clear here at the scene that Dr. Bob Crosby, for an unknown reason, stuck a gun in his mouth and pulled the trigger. "Honey, Bob committed suicide."

"Bob Crosby did not kill himself," she said angrily. "And if he did, then he had someone forcing him to do so."

"Was there anything in his past that might have caused him to do this?"

"His past?" He heard a siren wailing in the background. "What are you getting at Mike?"

He shuffled some papers nervously. "Well we found an e-mail on his home computer. Someone was threatening to expose something in his past."

He heard her breathing, rapidly and shallow. "I can't imagine what it could be."

A car door slammed and he heard a man's voice calling Kendall's name. "Is someone there with you?"

"Ah, yeah."

"Come on you can do better than." Jealousy hit him in the pit of his stomach. He'd acted all fine with the idea of Kendall seeing other men. That was before they'd been intimate. "Is that Johnnie Black I hear?"

"Yes, he called right after I left the ICU. I was a mess and he told me to wait here. That he was coming. And now, he's here."

This was really starting to piss him off. Yeah he'd been a jerk, but there was no reason to throw the guy in his face. He wanted to lash out, to strike her where she was least expecting it. "Oh one more thing."

"Yes?" she said expectantly.

"Dr. Crosby's final ruling on Carpenter's death was found on his desk. Here let me read it to you." He turned to the last page. "My findings are conclusive. Cheona Carpenter died of an accidental heroin overdose."

He heard her gasp into the phone. "You know that's not true Mike."

He laughed. "And about your little fantasy that Carpenter was pregnant..." Turning to page three he continued, "The uterus is normal in size, no evidence of disease or pregnancy."

"What?" She mumbled something to Johnnie. "I was there Mike. I saw the uterus. He cut it open in front of me and there was a small fetus inside. I don't know what the game is, but he's covering something up for someone. Listen to the autopsy tape Mike."

"Kendall we haven't found any tape. The autopsy report, however, is clear. This case is closed."

"Just like that?"

"Just like that."

"What should I do with your truck?" she said.

"Just leave it there with the keys under the mat. I'll have one of the guys drop me off. Enjoy your night with pretty boy."

He heard her say his name and hit the off button. She was unbelievable. One minute all into him and the next running to Black.

Then reality socked him hard in the gut. He was being a jerk again. How did he ever expect to regain Kendall's trust if he couldn't control himself? He dialed her number again.

"She doesn't want to talk to you Mike."

"Put her on Black."

"She's inside saying goodbye to the nurses."

"I can wait."

"Too bad I can't. Good night Mike. Better luck controlling your sparkling personality next time. Thanks for making me look so good."

The phone disconnected. "Damn it." He was blowing it again. Mike picked up the file. Kendall was no dope and if she said there was a fetus, then there was. The question was where did it go and who got rid of it?

Mike looked up as a Wayne police officer stepped in the conference room. "Officer Matt, did you find a tape of the autopsy performed today on Cheona Carpenter?"

"Tape sir?"

"Yes the medical examiner apparently records the audio of all autopsies performed. Was there one from today?"

Officer Matt shook his head. "There was a tape dated today but it was blank when we listened to it."

Mike sat back in the chair. "Blank, huh?"

"Yes sir." Officer Matt coughed. "Anything else you need?"

Mike shook his head. "No. Thank you for your help."

The young cop leaned against the doorframe. "Just why are the state troopers handling a simple break-in at the medical examiner's office?"

"How long have you been on the job son?"

"A little over a year," Matt said smugly.

Standing up Mike walked over to the other man. "One little word of advice son..."

The cop edged out the door.

"Sometimes simple break-ins really aren't simple at all. Why don't you take off? There are a few more things I need to go over. I'll secure the facility before I leave."

Meekly, the cop nodded and left.

Forty-eight

Mike stood staring at the computer screen. Things were off here, but when it came to computers he was an amateur. There had to be some way to trace the e-mail to Crosby's home computer. He picked up the phone and dialed the Totowa State Police Barracks. Phil Summers was a whiz with computers and would be thrilled to be reassigned from the dog of a case he was on now to this.

The dispatcher answered. "State Police Totowa Barracks."

"Good evening, this is Lt. Garcia. Please transfer me to Trooper Summers' line."

The phone rang several times before a gruff voice answered. "Trooper Summers."

"Phil, it's Mike. Can you come to the medical examiner's office in Wayne?"

"Now?"

"Yes, right away. I have a computer problem I need some help with."

"On my way,"

"Hey, Phil, wait a minute. My truck is sitting at St. Joe's ER. Could you get one of the road guys to drive you over there to pick it up for me?"

"Sure buddy, no problem. Are the keys in it?"

"She said she'd leave them under the mat."

"Oh shit...she?" said Phil. "She as in Kendall?"

"Am I that obvious?"

"I can't wait for you to fill me in. I'll be there soon."

Mike hung up the phone thinking of Kendall. He had to clear his head before Phil arrived. In the employee lounge he plugged a dollar bill into the soda machine and was rewarded with an ice-cold coke. Taking a sip, he walked back into the office planning to make good use of time until Phil arrived.

Something was right in front of his eyes. He felt it deep within himself. Turning back to page one of the Carpenter file he started to read. He'd find it no matter how long it took.

And he'd win Kendall back in the process. He fought the doubts creeping in because, face it, he was pushing forty.

His competition looked like one of the Arian race, perfect blonde hair, and buff body. Damn, even his teeth were sparkling white. He checked him out with the other cops: Twenty-seven and lives in his own mansion on the hundred-acre estate his family owns.

Hell, how could a trooper compete with that? He shook his head.

Kendall was no ordinary girl though. She never went for the trappings. She went for simple things. No Hollywood here.

Simple yeah. She was simply the best thing that ever happened to him, and he wasn't going to blow it again.

Pushing his feelings aside, he got back to the business at hand and began searching for anything that would throw some support Kendall's way. This investigation wasn't over. Not by a long shot. No matter what Crosby's autopsy report said.

Forty-nine

Kendall opened Mike's truck door throwing the keys on top of the mat. Let them steal it! From her purse she pulled out the tape. This is better than you deserve Mike, she thought. From behind, strong arms gripped her around her waist startling her.

Johnnie folded his arms around Kendall. Nuzzling his face in her hair, he inhaled her sweet scent. "Come here baby. Let me warm you up. It's freezing out there with all this rain. That's right baby, lean into me. Let me fill you up."

"Shit Johnnie, you scared me." Wiggling out of his embrace, she backed away from the truck with Johnnie following.

"Come here honey. I'm sorry I scared you." Slowly he lowered his lips to hers, brushing them lightly at first then more demanding. He felt her tense in his arms and backed away. "What is it baby?"

"Johnnie, please. You are being so nice, but I'm too upset to enjoy this right now." She pushed him away. "You got here so fast. Thanks."

He smiled, revealing even, white teeth, bought and paid for by dear, old dad. "I understand." He squeezed her shoulders. "You're coming to my place tonight."

Placing his arm around her back, he herded her to the waiting Mercedes. "Come on darlin'. Get in my car."

"Your place?" Sliding inside she slumped down in the seat as Johnnie got in on the driver's side. "Oh gee. I can't."

"Why not?" He leaned over, pulling her into his body. "I promise nothing will happen if you don't want it to." He pulled up her chin and kissed her softly.

"Don't you get it? I respect you and I care for you more than you know. You, Ms. Rose, are so refreshingly different from anybody I've ever dated. I won't do anything to ruin this relationship." He held up his hand. "Scout's honor."

She smiled. "I believe you. But I still have to go home."

"Why?"

"Someone with four legs and a stumpy tail is counting on me to be there."

He laughed. "Ole Bela girl. Well we'll just have to go pick her up now, won't we?"

"Really? You'd let her come to your house?"

"Of course. I love animals. Wait until you see my family's estate. It's crawling with every kind of four-legged creature you can think of. Bela will love it." He patted her leg. "We can even bring Max if you want."

Leaning back in the Mercedes seat she locked eyes with him. "And nothing will happen."

"What I said exactly was nothing will happen that you don't want to happen." He pointed at her. "You, Paramedic Rose, are in charge of this scene."

"In that case you've got yourself a deal. To be honest, with Tom away tonight, I was a little nervous about staying there alone. You know with all that's going on it's kind of spooky to live way out there."

Bending his pointer finger he said, "Come here you."

Exhausted by the day's events, she fell into his arms reveling in the closeness and warmth of his lean body.

"Tomorrow morning we can have breakfast with my father and step-mother. They can't wait to meet you."

"You've mentioned me to them?"

He turned the key bringing the lean Mercedes to life. Putting it in first, he headed out the parking lot, turning right onto Straight Street.

"Of course I did. You're very special to me."

She leaned back in the seat. "Well I hope I can live up to the advanced billing."

She looked behind her. "Guess I'll follow you in the Firebird seeing as how Bela weighs a hundred pounds and there is no back seat."

Black laughed merrily. "You can always ride on the roof."

She smacked his arm. "Me!"

"Well you don't expect me to put someone as beautiful and delicate as Bela out in the elements, do you?"

Smiling, she turned up the radio. "You, Mr. Black, are incorrigible."

Hitting the gas he merged onto route 80 west. The roads were slick with rain, but the Mercedes clung to the blacktop like it was a second skin.

"I really do care about you." He squeezed her hand. "I know we haven't been together long, yet I feel this connection to you I can't even explain."

She squeezed his hand back. "I care about you too, Johnnie, but it is way too early to be thinking seriously. Plus there's still Mike."

"Mike," he said sharply. "What do you see in that guy?"

"Sometimes I wonder," she said softly. She looked out the window. "It sure has turned cold tonight."

"Ah, changing the subject Ms. Montague?"

"Yup," she said.

"Someday you're going to have to make a choice. You can't keep dating both of us."

"Why not? I'm not interested in getting married. Plus guys do it all the time."

"I'm a reformed ladies man." He tapped his chest using his pointer finger. "Thanks to you."

"I'll believe it when I see it. I've asked a few other cops about you and you have quite the reputation."

He jerked the Mercedes sharply onto the shoulder and stopped. Turning to Kendall he took her hand in his. "People can change. Surely you believe that?"

Eighteen-wheelers roared by them, kicking up water and gravel that hit the sports car like hail.

"Johnnie, it isn't safe to park here. Come on let's get going," she said nervously.

He stared at her coldly. "Not until you tell me you believe I could change for you."

Johnnie's green eyes sparkled with something she couldn't place. Was he enjoying her fear or was he being serious? "Of course I believe you could change."

She leaned back against the window. "But if you don't get this car moving right now there won't be a reason to change. I don't like to be intimidated or put in dangerous positions."

Black grinned flashing his white teeth. "My, you are a vixen." Putting the Mercedes in gear, he waited for a clearing in traffic and pulled back onto route the highway.

"You know we could have gone a shorter way," said Kendall.

"Why rush when we can spend time together?" Black got off route 80 onto route 23 in Wayne.

Kendall took the time to study him. Johnnie was one of the most handsome men she'd ever seen. His profile was strong and chiseled. Tanned skin offset his striking blonde hair. She wanted to reach out and touch his biceps bulging out from his short-sleeved shirt. There wasn't any fault she could find. He could easily have any woman he wanted and by some accounts already had.

Yet, despite everything, he didn't hold a candle to Mike. No matter what she did she couldn't forget him; couldn't stop loving him.

Pulled from her thoughts she heard Johnnie speaking softly. "So whom exactly have you been asking about me?" Changing quickly to the fast lane, the Mercedes cut a path through the water throwing water up on all sides.

"Some of the Wayne cops I'm friendly with."

Squinting sharply at her, he said gruffly, "You know, I really need my privacy." Reaching over he squeezed her leg.

"Hey. That hurts." She slapped his hand away. "Cut it out."

He laughed sweetly. "Sorry honey. I didn't mean to pinch that hard." He turned back to the road. "My family worries about things like that."

Pushing back in the seat she glared him. "Like what Johnnie? My asking a few people about the new man I'm dating." She shook her head. "If you're expecting me to be a sophisticated, perfectly coifed woman, you're with the wrong girl. What you see is what you get."

A smile formed in the corner of his mouth. "That's not what I'm expecting at all. I like you just the way you are. Warts and all."

She smacked his arm. "Warts huh?"

"Seriously, I'm only trying to prepare you for meeting the family. I've never quite been able to fit in with the mighty Blacks. Maybe that's why I'm so attracted to you?"

"Ah, the family rebel," she said.

Turning into the Victorian's driveway, the Mercedes splashed through the puddles coming to a stop at Kendall's apartment door.

"It will only take me a few minutes to get things together. Come on up."

Trotting up the steps, she walked inside and screamed.

Fifty

He stared at the paper before him. So there had been a specimen sent out last night. Picked up at five PM.

He dialed the number on the slip. "Damn. The office is closed until tomorrow morning." He slammed down the phone. He glanced up to find Phil Summers staring at him from the doorway.

"Hey there handsome," he said.

"Hey yourself," said Mike. He leaned back in the chair. "This is the baby I need you to break." He tapped the computer screen.

Mike got up and motioned for Phil to take the chair.

"Thanks for getting me re-assigned. The case I was on blowed." Phil's silver hair glistened in the brightly lighted room. "This should be no problem."

He tapped the keys quickly. "You mentioned that Crosby received a threatening e-mail at home."

Mike nodded, leaning over Phil's back. "Yes."

"Well I can tell you it came from this computer."

"What?"

Phil pointed to the screen. "Right here. It shows this computer was on-line a little before 6:30 and sent e-mails to Crosby's house."

"Well I'll be damned. Kendall was right," said Mike.

"Right about what?"

"Somebody lured Crosby down here and forced him to kill himself." Mike pounded the table with his fist. "Damn it!"

"That's stretching it a bit, isn't it Mike?" said Phil sympathetically. "I know you still have strong feelings for Kendall but..."

"But nothing. I'll bet my career on this one Phil."

Phil swiveled in the chair and looked up at Mike. "Well that's saying something. OK, if you feel that strongly let's get to work. You'd be amazed how much the hard drive of a computer can tell."

Mike tapped Phil's back. "Thanks buddy."

"No problem." His hand brushed his coat pocket. "Hey, I almost forgot." He pulled out a micro-cassette tape. "I found it on the driver's seat of your truck."

Mike took the cassette from Phil. "There has to be one here somewhere," he said, opening drawers to the desk.

"You mean one of these?" Phil held up a micro-cassette recorder. "I always keep one on hand."

Mike placed the cassette inside and hit play. As if from the dead, Dr. Bob Crosby's voice filled the room.

"Passaic County case 02-6034," Sitting in a chair next to Phil, Mike listened to Crosby's detailed recording of the autopsy.

Fifty-one

After dinner CJ wished the night didn't have to end so soon. So when he suggested they go somewhere to talk, she happily followed him to the local park.

She got out of the Viper, running through the raindrops to Andy's car. Opening the passenger door, she slipped in beside him. She couldn't remember a time she'd been so attracted to a man she just met. She wished she'd dressed up a bit more, but how could she have known she'd meet the man of her dreams in Kendall's kitchen?

Mesmerized by his dark good looks, she watched his mouth move without hearing a sound.

"CJ?" he said.

"Sorry I was just lost in thought."

His teeth flashed beneath a well-trimmed, brown mustache. "Blinded by my good looks eh?" he said teasingly.

"Actually I am, very much so."

His face turned a bright shade of red. "Really?"

"Really," she said shyly.

He put the car in park and leaned back against the window. "You didn't have to run to my car you know. I pride myself on being a gentleman."

CJ smiled. "I didn't want your hair to get wet."

He patted his crew cut. "Yes it does go so flat in the rain." Shyly he looked at CJ. "So, would you like to go out again? Maybe a dinner or movie?"

"I'd love to," she said.

He let out a relieved whoosh of air. "Well who would have figured I'd meet a beautiful girl, third party, through an ambulance request?"

He tapped the wheel. "Speaking of Garrison, I'm worried about you and Kendall."

"Why? I thought he was on a respirator in ICU?"

"He is. But we don't know what was behind the assault, and that concerns me."

"You think we might be in danger?" CJ asked warily.

"Look, I don't want to panic you." He took her hand in his. "I just want you and Kendall to be alert and to tell me anything unusual that goes on."

She nodded. "We'll be careful. Right now I'm following up a lead regarding Jack Garrison."

"Garrison's kid?"

"Yes. We believe that is who Mark Garrison was implicating before he collapsed. The other son, Billy, he's too young and seemed a little slow to me." She reached over and touched his hand. "So will you join our posse?"

"Posse?"

"Yes. Kendall and I feel very strongly that Cheona Carpenter was murdered. We're not going to stop until we find out the truth." Holding his gaze she said, "We could use all the help we can get."

"Hum." He lifted her hand to his lips and kissed it softly. "I'm at your disposal Ms. Wagner," he said with a yawn.

Smiling brightly she tasseled his hair with her fingers. "You had better get some sleep." Opening the door she got out.

"Hey I might be tired, but I still have manners." He pushed open his door, jumped out and met her by the passenger door. "Let me walk you to your car."

They stepped two feet to the left. "Well here we are," she said, laughing.

Andy opened the Viper's door. CJ slid inside and lowered the window. "Thank you kind sir."

Leaning against the door he lowered himself through the window and kissed her lightly on the lips. "Call you tomorrow." He winked and was gone.

CJ sat there stunned. Could this really be happening? Had a gorgeous cop just kissed her with the promise of more to come? Turning the key, she revved the powerful engine and drove home to tell her mother.

Fifty-two

"It can't be. Oh please no!" She held the lifeless body of Max, her tomcat. "Why would somebody do this? He's just an innocent animal!"

Bela sniffed the body of her friend and whined. Kendall stroked the dog's soft face. "I'm sorry honey."

Johnnie stood on the stairs examining the noose. "Plain and simple. It's a warning."

He sat on the stairs next to Kendall stroking Max's soft orange fur. "I'm so sorry baby." He tipped her head up. "Look at me honey. This isn't a game anymore!"

Tear-filled eyes met his.

"You have to promise me that you and CJ will stay out of this now and let us cops do our jobs."

"No," she said forcefully.

"No?" He squeezed her chin. "Don't you get it? This is a warning that you'll be next. First Garrison, then Crosby, and now your cat. It's escalating!"

"Yeah, well, it's not only escalating it's now personal. Fuck him!" Hugging Max to her chest she got up and walked outside.

"Where are you going?" said Johnnie, following behind.

"To bury my cat. That's where!" She yanked open the barn door and fumbled for the light switch, tears running down her face. "Oh Maxie."

Johnnie raced up beside her and put his hands on her shoulders. "Honey let me do that." He flipped on the light, gently taking Max from her hands.

She let go without a struggle. "Damn him! Why hurt an innocent animal? Coward! I wish he would come after me."

"Don't even say that in jest," Johnnie said.

"I mean it. To hurt a person is one thing. But kill a trusting animal. He has no idea what he's just unleashed."

"Where?" Johnnie asked sympathetically.

She stood up. "I think under the shade tree in the cow field. He used to lay there during the summer heat."

Johnnie carried the cat outside and Kendall followed, lighting the way with a flashlight. The rain was falling heavier now, soaking them both to the skin.

Under the large tree Kendall cradled Max, while Johnnie dug his grave. He reached out. "Here baby. Give him to me."

She didn't want to let go of the ten year old. To do so would mean he was really gone.

Gently Johnnie pried her fingers open and lifted the cat from her. He laid the cat in the hole. "I'm so sorry Kendall."

She knelt by the open grave. "Maxie you were the most special cat in the world. We really went through a lot together and I'm so very sorry I wasn't there when you needed me." She broke down, her body heaving with tears.

"It wasn't your fault Kendall. You didn't know this would happen. How could you? Go inside honey. I'll finish here." He lifted her up with his strong arms. Kissing her sweetly he pushed her to go.

Head down, she walked slowly across the field with Bela at her side. She went inside to pack for Johnnie's. She didn't care if she ever came back to this place.

Looking out the window she watched her knight in shining armor kneeling at the grave. His lips moved quickly, but she couldn't make out what he was saying as he shoveled the last bit of dirt over the grave and packed it down with his foot.

"Thank you Johnnie for so much. You are a sincere guy after all. I do believe you are someone who'd be good for me."

She bent down and gathered up Bela's toys and food bowl. Ten minutes later she drove away, behind the Mercedes, without bothering to glance back at the towering Victorian on the hill.

Fifty-three

CJ's father met her at the door. "Where have you been?" he asked sharply.

"Dad. What's wrong?"

He placed his arm around her shoulders. "Honey I'm sorry, it's almost midnight. Your mother and I have been worried about you."

"I was out with Kendall. What's going on?"

He handed her a computer-generated note. "This was slipped under the door earlier tonight."

She read the note, startled by its contents. "Maybe Andy's right?"

"Who's Andy?"

"Dad sit down; we need to talk." She motioned toward the couch then sat in the plush leather chair across from it. "The other day Kendall and I were sent to do a pronouncement in Willow Run. When we got there we were told it was a suicide by heroin overdose."

CJ's father coughed. "But."

"But things didn't add up to us and we've made no secret of the fact we think the woman was murdered. Little things have happened, we think, in an attempt to scare us."

"I'm calling my security team immediately," said Mr. Wagner. "Give me the note honey."

She handed him the paper. "Dad, do you really think that's necessary?"

He shot her a look. "Yes honey I do. My little girl isn't going to get hurt by some maniac." He picked up the phone and dialed. "I think you had better call Kendall and let her know what's going on."

CJ nodded and headed upstairs to her room where she had a private phone line. First she called Kendall's home phone and left a message when there was no answer. Next she called her cell. Kendall picked up on the second ring.

"Hello."

"Kendall it's CJ. There's been a development."

"CJ! My gosh, I've been trying to reach you for the last hour. Bob Crosby's on life support at Joe's. They say he shot himself over some threatening e-mail and Max has been murdered."

"Oh no. Where are you?"

"Johnnie's taking Bela and I to stay at his house. We're on Route 23 now."

"You're going to Willow Run?"

"Yes." Bela barked in the background. "Easy girl," said Kendall.

"Ask Johnnie if I can come over. I really have to talk to you."

"Actually I'm following him right now. I'm sure it will be OK. Meet us at his house in fifteen minutes. Do you know where it is?"

CJ laughed softly. "Everybody knows where the Blacks live."

She hung up the phone and changed into blue jeans and a maroon sweater. The weather remained cold and damp with heavy drizzle.

Trotting down the stairs, she went to where her dad sat talking on the phone. She placed an arm around his shoulder and squeezed it.

He held the phone from his ear. "Are you going out?"

"Yes, to meet Kendall at Johnnie Black's house in Willow Run."

"Black? He's involved in this too?"

She nodded her head. "Up to his eyebrows."

"One of my men will follow you over to make sure you get there safely." He reached out for her hand then kissed her palm. "Be careful sweetheart. I'll keep working on this end to find out what I can."

She smiled. "Thanks Dad. I love you." She scooped up her keys and headed out to the Viper.

From the five-car garage another vehicle started up and followed her slowly down the drive.

Fifty-four

"Wow!" said Mike, shutting the tape off. "Damn, she *was* pregnant. Kendall was right. I've been such an ass."

Phil shrugged. "So now what?"

"First promise me you'll never let me send Trooper Monroe to an autopsy ever again." Mike laughed softly.

Phil nodded. "Man, did you get a load of how loud that kid can puke?" He pulled the keyboard out again. "Let me get back to work on this."

"Phil I know something is here and we're just missing it. I can feel it in my gut."

"I think you're right and we won't stop until we find it." Phil tapped the keys quickly.

Mike leaned over his shoulder watching. He pointed to the screen. "Does this say the e-mail was sent from this office to his home computer an hour before he shot himself?"

"Yes. That's how it's shaping up." Phil continued tapping on the keyboard. "It looks like somebody tried to erase all the files, but they never met ole Phil before." He hit a key then sat back in the chair with a triumphant grin. "There you go."

On the screen appeared Crosby's files for the past six months.

"Can you show me the Carpenter file?"

"Sure can." He pulled up the file. "It doesn't look like much was entered before he died."

Mike bent over to look at the screen scanning the rough draft of the autopsy report. "There has got to be something here." He hit the desk with the palm of his hand. "Damn it Crosby, speak to me."

Phil scrolled the report down. "Didn't you say Carpenter was twenty two?"

"Yes," said Mike.

"Says here she's a twenty seven year old male."

"Must be a typo." Mike scanned the report. "Let's see if anything else is out of place. Kendall swore the girl was pregnant and she was right. She also swore Crosby left before he entered anything in the computer."

He pulled on latex gloves. Bending down, he pulled a half burned file folder from the metal wastebasket. "Looks like our boy set a little fire. So how come the alarms didn't go off?"

Phil held up an empty bottle of water. "Might be he put it out before they did."

Mike scanned the ceiling his eyes settling on the remnants of the hard-wired smoke detector. "Or some creative destruction of the alarm system. This guy is good."

"Smart too," said Summers.

"What was the case number Crosby read on the tape?" Mike rewound the tape and listened to Crosby's voice play. "Passaic County case 02-6034."

Hitting "stop" he looked at the screen.

"Well the audio matches the computer input, PCC# 02-6034." Phil looked up expectantly. "Why?"

"It's the same on this burnt file." Mike rubbed his chin. "I thought I saw another number on the last page of the computer file."

Phil scrolled to the bottom of the file, last page and nodded. "You're right. They are in bold print and underlined: 25225 343 48. Wonder what they mean?"

"Nothing goes with them anywhere in the file? Maybe they signify a lab slip or organ number?" Mike said.

"Not according to anything I have here on the screen. The lab number doesn't match. I don't see anywhere that he numbered the organs from the autopsy like that."

Eyes down, Mike stared blankly, landing on the phone. Slowly he spelled each number out according to the buttons. "Wait a minute." He grabbed a pen, writing the numbers down with a furious pace.

"What have you got?"

"I think it's a code."

Phil wrote the numbers down on another sheet. "How are we gonna break it?"

Mike jutted his chin at the phone. "Could it be that simple?"

Methodically the two men worked the numbers, comparing letters with numbers. Simultaneously Mike and Phil exhaled.

"Holy shit!" said Mike.

"Did you come up with what I did?"

"We have to find Kendall. Now!"

Phil jumped up, grabbed his jacket and raced with Mike to a marked cruiser parked outside.

"Call for another ride troop," Mike said as he raced by the trooper stationed at the door.

Fifty-five

CJ knocked on the door. The home was big and imposing, more like an ancient castle in Ireland than a home to one family.

She waved off her father's security man idled at the curb. He waved then drove away. She'd call him when she wanted to leave and, like a good security guy, he'd escort her back home. She felt silly, yet at the same time grateful and safe.

She rang the bell this time. Black's Mercedes was in the garage. She glanced back and noticed the Firebird parked beside the enormous garage. Good, Kendall was here.

She shivered as a cold, howling wind hit her exposed face. Behind her the rattling bushes startled her. Turning around quickly, fear shot through her heart.

"Who's there?" she called loudly.

Squinting through the rain, she scanned the area. Hair on the back of her head bristled, and her heart rate kicked up. Pounding her fist on the door she knocked again and hit the doorbell twice. "Come on!"

The door opened slowly, illuminating Johnnie Black's face. Relief coursed through her as she smiled back at him.

Fifty-six

"Johnnie, was that CJ at the door?" called Kendall.

"No honey. It was her father's man with a note." He handed the note with blue ink script. "Seems she can't make it."

"Her father's what?" Kendall scanned the note. "Something isn't right. She just called me."

"I know. But read it yourself."

"I am." She shook her head, pulling her cell phone from her purse. "Let me just give her a call and make sure she's OK."

Glancing up she saw a grin covering Johnnie's face, which he quickly masked. "I'm sure she's fine."

"What are you smiling at Johnnie?"

"I think it's cute how you worry about people you care about. Hopefully I'll be one of them soon."

Her face softened. "You're getting there Black." She smiled.

"No answer. It went right to voice mail." She left a message for CJ to call her. "Let me call her parents-"

Black took the phone from her hand, squeezing it hard. "Later," he said gruffly, leading her into a bathroom the size of her living room.

Mirrors lined the two far walls. Across from the door sat a huge tub with lit candles surrounding the sparkling water. "CJ's fine honey. I'm sure she'll be here any minute."

Kendall pulled her arm free. "I'm sure you're right Johnnie." Glancing around the room she walked over to the tub. "This bath is something I imagined in my dreams. It's beautiful Johnnie."

He pulled her into his embrace. "It's yours from now on. If you'll have me."

She pulled away and looked him in the eyes. "We've only known each other a short time. Let's not rush things."

Kissing him lightly on his full lips, she saw a flash of anger glint in his eyes. Deepening her kisses, she trailed her arms down his defined back and stopped above his buttocks.

Lust replaced the anger as Johnnie matched her desire. He cupped her breasts, kneading them roughly. "I want you Kendall."

She licked his ear. "Not yet handsome."

"Don't tease me." He bit her earlobe. "I hate teases!" He whispered, menacingly.

A nagging fear filled her. "Johnnie stop. I'm not ready to go any farther." Tensing up she struggled to pull away.

He squeezed her tightly. "Wait. I won't do anything you don't want me to." He released his vise-like grip, shaking his head and smiling. "Damn. You are the first woman I've ever respected enough to..."

He stopped talking. Taking her hand he led her to the tub, filled with hot, perfumed water.

"I drew this bath for you." He kissed her lips, slowly unbuttoning her shirt. "Nothing you don't want," he whispered softly.

She wondered when had he had time to run her a bath?.

His hands undid the last button on her shirt and he slipped it off her shoulders watching it fall to the floor.

Johnnie knelt, his blonde hair glistening in the fire's light. Gazing at her with a questioning look, he tentatively touched the top of her jeans. "May I?"

Part of her wanted to say no, the other half felt free, wild, flattered that such a young, handsome man wanted her this much.

Seconds later the jeans lay in a heap at her feet. Johnnie stood up. "I've got to check on the horses," he said, his voice void of emotion.

He edged her toward the tub. "You get in there and soak all your cares away."

Caught off guard by his demeanor, Kendall stood for a moment, staring at the door. What the heck is going on? She hesitated by the tub unsure what to do.

Johnnie ran his hands up her backside to her bra clasp, undoing it slowly. "You are so beautiful," he said softly. Pulling the bra off her shoulders he let it drop, cupping her pert breasts with his large hands. "Perfect size. Um." Kneading her breasts he kissed her deeply. "Take your panties off now Kendall!" he ordered.

Freaked out by his constant changing demeanor, she couldn't move. His hands ran down her abdomen pulling her panties with them. She stood before him vulnerable.

Pushing her back toward the tub, he said sweetly. "I won't be long baby. Now please get in the tub."

Under his watchful eye, she slipped into the warm water, laying her head on a bath pillow. "Thank you," he said.

Splashing the water with his hand, he turned on the massage jets, churning the water to life. Suds began to build up surrounding her body in foam.

She thought of the 9mm Glock she'd stashed in her purse. Could she use it against another living being? The time she and Bobbie had spent at the range had given her the confidence she'd needed with a gun. Her aim had only gotten better the more time she spent at the shooting range. Imagining Mike's face as her target hadn't hurt either.

Mike filled her mind more and more lately. Johnnie was young, handsome, and flattering, but Mike was still the love of her life, no matter how much she fought it.

She looked up to find Johnnie gone. Somewhere outside a door slammed, followed by what she thought was a muffled scream.

Rising to her knees in the tub she looked out the bay window surrounding it. Outside the wind screeched, pitching trees back and forth through a misty rain. She lay back down in the tub. Must be the wind. Leaning back she flicked on the bathroom TV going to the news. Maybe something about Bob would be on. Turning the volume up she relaxed, wondering if she was making too much of Johnnie's attitude.

Twenty minutes passed. What was taking him so long to finish up the horses? Unable to shake the feeling something was very wrong, she stood up in the tub, looking out through the dismal, rainy night.

Fifty-seven

Wherever she was, it was dark. Outside wind and rain beat against the structure with a terrible force.

Her hands were tied above her head. Her legs spread eagle, nylon rope tethering her ankles to the table. Her clothes had been removed, neatly folded and set on a chair. Above her a low watt light bulb swung in the breeze whipping through the room.

Surely Kendall and Johnnie would come looking for her when she didn't show up. Memories converged on her mind. She had shown up. She'd seen Johnnie's face smiling at her from the doorway, then nothing.

Somewhere a door slowly squeaked open. Like an animal caught in a trap, she struggled against the restraints. She wasn't gonna die like this!

Rope cut into her wrists, searing through the flesh. Flinging her arms and legs she screamed against the duct tape covering her mouth. Aware she wasn't alone. Behind her someone giggled softly.

Her right wrist felt looser, nearly free. Ceasing the struggle she waited for her captor to appear. At least now she might be able to make a stand. Beside her, a shadow crossed the floor then stood before her.

No! It couldn't be.

Smiling, he ripped the duct tape off her mouth. "You know I've always been attracted to you. He inhaled her scent deeply. Caressing her cheek with his hand he lowered his mouth covering hers.

Pulling away she spat. "Why are you doing this?"

Smiling he bite her lip lightly and stood up. "Why sweet thing? That's simple. Because we can."

Trailing his hand down her neck he cupped her breast, playing with the nipple between his thumb and pointer finger. "Bet that feels good."

"Don't!" she cried. "I thought you wanted Kendall?"

Releasing her breast, he lightly touched her stomach, moving down to her thick black triangle. "Are you ready for me yet, honey?" He dipped his fingers inside her.

Her body tensed. "Stop it Johnnie it's not funny anymore. Let me go and I swear I won't tell Kendall."

Pulling his finger out he lifted it to his mouth, sniffing it as he slowly licked it with his tongue. "Um, yummy. I knew you'd taste good." He exhaled loudly and walked up to her head.

"You just don't get it yet, do you?"

Her eyes widened as she watched him slowly unbutton his jeans. "Don't do this Johnnie."

"Johnnie," he laughed softly.

The last button undone he pushed down his jeans revealing his engorged manhood. "If you're a good girl, I'll loosen one hand so you can touch it." Encircling his cock with his hand he stroked it up and down.

"I'll never understand how women can be so stupid."

"Oh we're far from stupid Johnnie."

Releasing his cock he leaned over her, his face inches from hers. "Then why do you keep calling me Johnnie?"

Lifting his legs he stepped out of his pants, and then lowered himself onto CJ. "Can't you see yet?" He sat on her stomach, unbuttoning his shirt. "I'm not Johnnie."

"You need help Johnnie. Just stop this now and nothing will happen to you. Johnnie I swear..."

"He's right you know," said a male voice from behind her. "How can he be Johnnie?" He walked in front of her. "When I am?"

"Shall we turn on the TV brother?" Johnnie asked. "We can watch our next one making herself all clean for us."

Suspended above the table a TV came on, brightly revealing Kendall in the bath. "Now do you get it?" said Tommy.

"Why are you doing this to us?" CJ started to cry. "We've never done anything to you."

"Oh haven't you?" said Johnnie. "If you'd just have kept your pretty little noses out of it, this never would have happened." He cackled, running his eyes up and down CJ's body. "But seeing as it has, we might as well enjoy ourselves."

Johnnie stood before CJ, pulling off his white tee shirt. "I know you want me CJ." Unzipping his black jeans he let them fall to the floor. He stood before her naked and flaccid.

As you can see I'll need a little extra effort on your part. He released her left hand and molded it around his cock. "Come on now let's see what you can do." He moved her hand up and down until he started to get hard.

"What are you waiting for little brother?"

"Please don't do this," cried CJ. Tommy positioned himself between her legs. The tip of his cock pressing against her opening. "No!"

"Remember the way Cheona used to beg us to do her at the same time," said Tommy.

"She was the best whore we ever had," said Johnnie. He looked at his hard cock, then at CJ's mouth. "Why don't you go first little brother? I'll have a little fun until you're done." Leaning over the table he pushed his manhood into CJ's mouth.

Gagging, crying she felt the brother enter her and begin to thrust. Staring at Kendall on the screen she retreated to her mind until only her body was there. Get out of there Kendall. Please. If there's any way I can make things up to you then hear this plea from me to you. Get out.

Fifty-eight

Cold bristled up her spine, causing the hairs on the back of her neck to stand up. Something was wrong. Where was Johnnie? It has been over forty minutes since he left.

She rose from the tub and stepped out; drying her body with the plush green towel he'd left her. She blew out the candles, slowly retreating into the bedroom.

Gathering her clothes she put them on quickly. Wrapping the leather holster around her ankle, she secured the Glock, and drew her pant leg over it.

Pulling on her ankle-high cowboy boots, she scoured the room for anything that might point to what was going on. There had to be something that would tell her more about Johnnie Black who, she had to admit, was acting stranger by the minute.

One thing that being a paramedic had taught her was to trust her gut instinct or her spidey senses as CJ liked to call it. And her gut was screaming.

The room itself, now that she looked at it, was dark and uninviting. On the dresser there were two sets of Stetson aftershave. She picked up a bottle. "Must really like the stuff."

Opening the top drawer of his dresser she rifled through it, shuddering with the realization where she'd seen something before. One cuff link lay hidden under clothing, and she knew where the other one was. It had caught her eye, but not registered at the time. Damn it! The dealer at the projects! That's where she'd seen it flashing at her from his shirt. What the hell was going on?

She walked back into the bathroom and opened the medicine cabinet over the sink. Inside hundreds of prescription bottles stared back at her. Elavil, Effexor, Valium, Vicodin. Shit, the guy was a psyche case with his own friggin' pharmacy.

"Bela, let's get the heck out of here. This place is giving me the creeps with a capital K."

She had to get hold of Mike. She pulled her cell phone from her purse and turned it on. The message alert sounded. Ignoring it she dialed Mike's cell phone. When nothing happened she glanced at the phone. "How can there be no cell sites?"

Picking up the house phone she started to punch Mike's number. No dial tone! She patted her leg. Come on girl let's go."

The yellow lab bounded to her side. Leaving Bela's things and her overnight bag where they lay, the two of them headed for Firebird.

Opening the door cautiously she held her hand for Bela to wait. Outside the wind blew whipping the rain into frenzy. "OK girl, the coast is clear."

Together they raced to the Firebird. Her hand shook trying to get the key into the lock. She screamed as a cold, wet hand covered hers.

Fifty-nine

"Baby where are you going?" said Johnnie, concern filling his voice. Placing his hands on her upper arms he turned her to face him. Lowering his face to hers, he kissed her gently.

Kendall recoiled as the smell of another woman filled her senses. "Where were you Johnnie?"

"I'm sorry I took so long. I had a little trouble with a mare I had to take care of. Everything's fine now."

Lifting her hand to his lips he kissed it gently. "I have a surprise for you."

Looking at him skeptically she said, "Oh yeah?"

"Yes. But it's not here." He slipped the key into the lock. "Go ahead get in you're getting wet."

She hesitated. "Where are we going?"

"To my grandfather's estate." He pointed out the drive. "It's just up the road." He looked at her sweetly. "Please come. I promise you won't be disappointed."

"Bela too?"

Johnnie stroked the dog's head. Bela growled softly. "Easy girl. I have a surprise for you too." He moved the driver's seat lever letting the dog into the back seat. "Your turn," he said to Kendall.

Getting in quickly, she shut the door and hit redial on her phone. Please let Mike be there she prayed. The phone beeped with a message alert as Johnnie slipped into the passenger seat.

"Who are you calling, honey?"

She kept it open and slipped it into her purse. "Nobody baby. There's a voice mail on it I haven't listened to yet. I'll get it later." She winked. "After my surprise."

Johnnie flashed his straight teeth. "That's my girl."

From the corner of her eye she saw CJ's car sticking out from the side of the garage. CJ where are you? Johnnie hadn't noticed. He was too busy telling her how to get to his grandfather's house.

"So what street does your grandfather live on?"

"Oh sweetie, my grandfather has been dead for years. He had a kick-ass house on one hundred prime acres. Worth a fortune." He patted his chest. "Hopefully soon to be mine."

"Is it on Melody lane?"

"It's just down the road a bit. Start driving. I'll tell you where to go."

"What's the address?"

He turned to her frowning. "Why so many questions?" he snapped.

She shrugged. "Sorry. Just curious, that's all. No need to get your panties in a bunch."

He ran his fingers down her cheek. "That's what I like about you Kendall, your spunk. Don't worry about the address baby. Worry about how excited you'll be in a few minutes."

"Worry Johnnie?"

"Wrong choice of words." Playfully he squeezed her thigh. "Think about how happy you'll be." Leaning over he kissed her neck lightly and blew softly into her ear. "Soon you'll be mine."

Braking, she stopped idling in the middle of the street. "Yours? What do you mean by yours?"

Over the top of the middle console he took her hand in his. Facing her he said. "You must realize by now that I'm crazy about you. My life was nothing before you came along."

She pulled her hand free. "We've only been seeing each other for a short time Johnnie." From the back seat Bela growled. "Easy girl." Rubbing the dog's head she struggled, trying to stall for time. Please be on the way Mike, she prayed. Putting the car in park she leaned into him. "I'll admit we have a special connection."

Johnnie threw the car back in drive. "Come on let's go. It's dangerous to sit in the middle of the road!" He pointed to the next street. "Make a right here." Silent, brooding he looked out the window.

Reaching over she fondled his upper leg to take down his guard. "Don't be mad at me Johnnie."

Looking down at her hand he grinned and pushed it onto his groin. "See what you do to me."

She felt his hardness growing beneath her palm. What the hell was she getting herself into? Face it; she couldn't count on Mike to show up like the cavalry. Cop or not, this guy was nuts. She had to come up with her own plan. And where was CJ?

"You are so sexy Johnnie." Rubbing him through his jeans she slowed the car, crawling along at a snail's pace.

"Turn here baby."

Through the passenger window she saw two crumbling stone pillars marking the entrance to the estate. "Wow, those white stone pillars sure look old. Is this your grandfather's place?"

"I'll have them torn down as soon as it's mine. Won't be long now."

She drove the Firebird up the winding drive. The windshield wipers beat away the pouring rain.

"Darn window," Kendall muttered. Pushing up on the driver's side window she struggled to get the glass back on track."

"What's the matter now?" said Johnnie.

"Ever since someone leaned on it a few months ago the window keeps slipping down. Not that it matters tonight. I'm soaked to the skin." She shivered rubbing her hands against her wet arms.

Johnnie rubbed her shoulder. "You'll be warm soon enough. I have a roaring fire and six course dinner waiting for you." He pointed up the hill at the French manor house with every light a blaze. "There she is. Beautiful isn't she?"

Kendall nodded. "Where should I park?"

"The drive's circular. Pull up right in front of the main door." Johnnie's hand was already opening the door before the Firebird came to a halt. He jumped out and raced around to Kendall's side, opening her door before she could hit the lock.

"Let's go sweetheart. You won't believe the fun that awaits you inside."

She stepped out, leaving the keys in the ignition. Bending down she started to release the seat.

Johnnie stopped her. "How about we bring Bela in later? I want you all to myself for a little while."

Before shutting the door Kendall loosened the driver's window. "Just let me give her a little air."

Johnnie nodded. Taking her hand he guided her up the stairs, stopping at the front door. "I believe this is where I carry you over the threshold." He swept her up into his arms.

This was getting weirder and weirder by the minute. How was she going to get away from this guy? She placed her arms around his neck, smiling sweetly.

Setting her down in the foyer he took her hand again and led her up a grand staircase. "Where are we going Johnnie?"

At the top of the landing she looked back hoping, praying to see a pair of headlights coming up the drive. Only darkness met her eyes. He pulled her into his arms. "I love you Kendall."

Releasing her with a kiss, he led her down a long hallway stopping before the last door. "In here awaits our future." He felt her hesitate. "What's wrong?" he asked angrily.

"Nothing honey. It's just that all this is so special." She kissed him lightly. "It's a little overwhelming actually."

"This is only the beginning. Once we start living here you'll never want for anything again."

The guy was nuts. She had to get out of here. Living here? What the hell was he talking about? She followed him into the master suite. Inside the room a hundred candles glowed. A trail of red rose petals covered the floor leading the way into the bedroom.

"The roses are a symbol of my love for you." Placing his hand in the center of her back he applied pressure, guiding her into the room. Before her was an ornate chair surrounded by candles. Behind it a king-size bed with fresh roses covering the white lace canopy.

"What's all this Johnnie?"

"Sit in the chair my darling." He pushed her down into the red velvet chair. Kneeling before her he took her hand in his. "I know we haven't known each other long, but from the first time I saw you I knew we were meant to be together."

Dizziness assailed her. "Johnnie," she whispered.

"Shh. Honey let me finish. Don't wreck the moment," he snapped.

He squeezed her hand tightly causing her to grimace with pain. "You're hurting me."

Relaxing the vise grip, he inhaled deeply. "I love you Kendall. I want to spend every day waking up next to you and every night wrapped in your arms as we fall asleep. You, a common woman, will become part of the most powerful family in the world. Kendall Black. Doesn't that sound wonderful?" He lifted her left hand up, pulling something out of his pocket.

Through wide eyes she watched him slip an enormous diamond onto her ring finger. "Kendall will you marry me?"

She swallowed deeply. "Johnnie, this is the most beautiful thing anyone has ever done for me."

"But?" he said angrily.

"But we hardly know each other. We need more time to..."

"I told you she was a lying whore," said a menacing voice from the shadows.

Kendall's eyes shot up. Before her knelt Johnnie and directly behind him stood his mirror image. "Who the hell are you?" What is going on?" She looked back and forth between the men.

"Who me? I'm just little ole Johnnie's brother. His twin as you can see." Walking toward her he leaned down. "I hope you're as good as your little friend CJ was. Nice piece of ass that one." He slipped his hand down her shirt squeezing her breast. "Yes, I think you'll do nicely."

"Stop it Tommy. She's mine. You said I could have her." Johnnie stood up facing off with his brother. "I've gone along with everything, but not this. I want her!"

Tommy gripped Johnnie's face between his hands. "Blood is thicker than pussy dear brother."

Johnnie started to cry, tears running down his face. His voice was that of a four-year-old child. "Why are you so mean to me Tommy? We always do what you want." He stomped his foot like a petulant child.

One inch at a time, Kendall angled her body away from the brothers locked in battle. Slowly she reached down.

"What do you think you're doing bitch?" shouted Tommy. Grabbing her hair he yanked her head up with such force it pulled her out of the chair. "You're not going anywhere, except to hell." He shoved her onto the bed.

It was the break she'd been looking for. Kicking out like a mule she caught Tommy in the groin with her boots. He fell to the floor holding his crotch.

Rolling off the bed, she fell onto the floor. Johnnie raced around the bed.

"Don't Johnnie" she said forcefully.

He lunged onto her as she leveled the Glock. A shot rang out striking the handsome blonde in the chest. Blood spurted across the room, covering the bed, and Kendall's jeans.

She pushed him off as he fell to the floor. "That one is for Maxie, you fucking bastard!"

Grabbing the corner post, she stood up pointing the gun wildly around the room as shadows flickered in the candle's light.

Edging her way toward the door she whipped the gun around firing at a menacing giggle behind her. Sudden blinding pain shot through her skull, dizziness swam before her. She felt herself falling into the abyss of unconsciousness and she saw no more.

Sixty

When she awoke she was tethered to the bed next to the body of Johnnie. Lifting her pounding head, she tried to focus her eyes on the form standing across the room.

Tommy stood beside a table mixing something, and then drawing it from a spoon into a syringe. Horror struck her as she realized what he intended to do. She pulled weakly against the nylon rope.

"Good. You're awake." He poured water over her head. "I want you to know exactly what's going to happen to you." His shoulders wracked with silent cries. "My brother—my baby brother—he's dead because of you, you fucking bitch!"

Pointing the Glock at her head, he pulled the trigger rapidly. "Damn gun. I'd love to fuck up your face like I did your little friend Dr. Crosby."

Downstairs a window broke. "They can come, but they'll never save you in time."

He rolled up her sleeve, slapping her arm to get a vein. Quickly he jabbed it in, drawing back until blood filled the syringe. Pushing the plunger down, he snarled. "So long you conniving cun..."

Bounding through the door, a yellow shadow leapt onto his back, biting, tearing at his body with brutal force. Tommy yelped in pain, kicking Bela in the abdomen. Barking and growling, she lunged at him grabbing his wrist with her teeth.

From his pants he pulled out a knife stabbing the dog. Bela fell, landing with a thud on the floor. She didn't get up.

"Bela! Not my dog you son of a bitch." Adrenaline coursed through her body, feeding her anger and strength. Ripping her arm free she pulled the needle out, knowing some of the drug had already entered her system. How long did it take for heroin to hit?

Leaning over she picked at the rope wrapped tightly around her hand. Shadows leapt across the room, dancing in the firelight.

A shot rang out. A body fell on top of her crushing her into the mattress. Arms were around her pulling her to the floor. Blackness crept into her, filling her mind with nothing. She could hardly take a breath. Breathe, I have to....

Sixty-one

Mike pinched her nose, sealing his mouth over hers and gave two deep breaths. "Come on Kendall. Fight it!"

Phil Summers raced into the room, followed by Andy Grey.
"The medics are on the way," said Phil.

"I can't find CJ anywhere," said Andy.

"One and two and three and four." Mike inhaled deeply then blew into Kendall's mouth. "Phil, check the dog. She's over by the bed."

Phil stepped over Mike and knelt down next to Bela. "She's still breathing," he said, scooping the dog into his arms. "I'm going to take her to the emergency vet clinic. Can you two handle this until back-up arrives?"

"Yes," said Andy. "Can I do anything to help you Mike?"

Mike gave Kendall another breath. "Go to my cruiser. In the trunk there is oxygen and a medical kit."

Andy ran out the door and down the stairs.

Mike silently thanked God Kendall had insisted he stock his cruiser with oxygen and first aid equipment, normally not carried by NJSP.

Phil shook his head. "I only wish we'd figured it out sooner. I'm really sorry Mike."

"She just needs some Narcan. Come on Kendall. Fight it!" He drew in a breath, exhaling into her mouth.

Andy raced back into the room out of breath, carrying the oxygen and first aid kit. "Where could CJ be?" said

Andy. "I'm really worried about her. Her father said she went over to Blacks."

Andy knelt down next to Kendall pressing his pointer and middle finger into her neck. "Her pulse is still strong and steady." He hooked up the pocket mask to oxygen and cracked open the life-giving green cylinder.

Between breaths Mike said, "Black doesn't live here Andy. He has a house on his father's estate."

Andy jumped up. "Then she's got to be there. I have to get a search warrant." He reached for the phone.

Mike gave Kendall another breath through the pocket mask. "Screw the search warrant. Go find your girl!"

"You're right. Can I take your car?" Andy looked out the window. "The medics just pulled up. I'll go direct them in." He reached down and squeezed Mike's shoulder. "Good luck buddy."

"Same to you." Mike watched him race out of the room. He bent down giving Kendall another breath. Only a few more minutes and he'd have her back. And he was never going to let her go again.

Heavy footsteps sounded on the stairs heralding the medic's arrival. "In here guys!" shouted Mike.

Bursting through the door, carrying the heavy blue med-bag, charged Paramedic Jerry Knight a thirteen-year veteran. Behind him followed Mack Taffy, a medic of one year.

Jerry ripped open an IV bag. "What happened Mike?"

Mike nodded at Tommy's body lying beside the bed. "He injected her with heroin. I don't know how much. She's been in respiratory arrest since I got here."

Mike grabbed the bag-valve mask Mack handed him and placed it over Kendall's face squeezing the bag to give a rush of oxygen into her lungs.

"What do you want me to do Jerry?" asked Mack with panic in his voice.

"I'll take care of Kendall." He pointed at the two bodies. "You check them."

Mack nodded and walked over to the handsome blonde lying on the bed. "This one's dead."

Jerry slapped on the tourniquet, tapping on Kendall's arm to raise a vein. "One thing this girl's got is good veins. Thank God," said Jerry, sliding the needle into her antecubital vein. He taped down the saline lock, hooked in the IV tubing and reached into the bag.

"I'll push the Narcan, which will block the heroin from getting into the cells. She should wake up in seconds, but you keep an eye on her. Narcan can make people vomit."

Mike gave Kendall another breath as he watched the medication flow out of the syringe and into her blood stream. "Come on honey. Start breathing."

Kendall took a slow breath, then another. Jerry hooked her up to the cardiac monitor and felt her radial pulse.

From the blue bag he pulled out a blood pressure cuff. "Looks like she's coming around," he said with relief in his voice. "Boy is she gonna owe me one."

Mike smiled. "You? I sucked face with her for twenty minutes before you got your butt here."

Kendall's eyes opened. "What happened?"

Mike helped her to a sitting position. "We saved your life that's all," he said tapping his chest.

"You came." She slipped her arms around Mike's neck, snuggling against his broad chest. Raising her face she kissed him on the lips.

"Whoa! Why don't you two get a room," said Jerry. "Ah after your trip to the ER." He knelt down next to Kendall.

"Jerry you're here too?" She took his hand in hers. "What's going on?" Suddenly she stiffened. "CJ!"

Pulling free from Mike she wobbled to her feet. "She's at Black's estate."

Mike eased her back into his arms. "Andy, along with the Willow Run police department, is on the way over there right now." He hugged her. "We don't know anything yet. You need to go to the hospital."

"No way." She pointed at Jerry. "Grab another Narcan mister cause we're going to find CJ. She may need you more than I do."

Mike shrugged, taking Kendall by the arm. "You and I both know there's no fighting her."

Jerry nodded, grabbing the med-bag. "Let's go!"

From the back of the room came a meek, "Am I going too?"

"Yes Mack. Of course you are. Did you get a strip on both the stiffs?"

"Actually one's not so stiff." He pointed. "I thought he was dead, but he isn't quite dead yet."

"What the hell. Why didn't you tell me?" Jerry shoved a Narcan syringe into Mike's hand. Quickly he disconnected the IV tubing from the saline lock and threw the bag of fluid on the floor. "It will be easier to travel with just a lock in her arm. If she starts getting groggy give her half of this through the saline lock." He pointed to the small clear tube taped to Kendall's arm. "Not too fast or she'll barf all over you. I've got to take care of him. I'll call for ALS 13 to meet you over at Black's estate."

Mike gave him directions for the other medic unit. Looking up he saw the chief of Willow Run police standing in the doorway. "Is it true?" said Fitzgerald.

"I'm afraid it is sir." He pointed at the medics. "They're working on one of the twins now, the other's dead."

"Twins?" said Chief Fitzgerald.

"Yes, they are brothers Johnnie and Tommy Black." Mike trailed Kendall out the door stopping at the puzzled look on the other man's face. "You mean you never knew he had an exact twin."

The chief shook his head. "No. But that certainly explains some strange things going on in the department." He held out his hand to Mike. "Thank you for everything Trooper Garcia."

Mike grasped the chief's hand, sheepishly shrugging as Kendall yelled for him to move it or lose it.

"Gotta go. Good luck. If you need anything here's my card. Call me."

Two uniformed officers ran up the stairs, their heavy combat boots announcing their arrival. Fitzgerald nodded at Mike then began issuing orders to his men.

Sixty-two

Kendall and Mike pulled up behind the arriving medic unit, ALS 13. The medics jumped out, and seeing Kendall in the cruiser they strolled over to her door.

She got out as Mike came around to join the group. "What have you got?" asked Paramedic Joe Corey.

Dizziness hit. She grabbed the car's mirror to steady herself. "Whoa."

Mike held out the syringe. "I think she might need some more of this."

Paramedic Bert Tolomo looked at the syringe. "What the hell?"

"I'll explain it to you later. Please just give her half of it like Jerry said!" Mike steadied Kendall with his hand.

Bert rolled his eyes showing Joe the syringe. "Since when is Kendall a user?"

"She isn't!" Mike grabbed Bert's arm roughly. "Just give it to her before she goes out again. I'll explain later."

"Please. I feel like hell." Her body swayed. She was going down.

Bert and Joe sprang to life. Joe grabbed an alcohol swab cleaning the IV port. Bert plunged the needle into it and slowly gave one milligram of Narcan.

"Easy girl," said Joe. "Sit her in the car."

Kendall stood up as the drug took effect. "No time to sit. CJ's on this estate somewhere. See there's her car." She pointed to the murky black area next to the garage.

"Let's see, I was taking a bath when I thought I heard screaming." She tapped her chin, scanning the house for the location of Johnnie's bathroom.

"Taking a bath?" said Mike angrily.

"Yes. Alone." Grabbing his sleeve she pulled him in the direction of the barn. "Johnnie said something about checking on the horses." She pointed at a large window on the second floor. "That's the bathroom up there so the barn has to be close by."

As they rounded the corner Andy Grey nearly collided with them. "We've searched the entire house and can't find her anywhere." Wiping the sweat from his brow he stopped to catch his breath. "We have to find her."

"Follow me before the Narcan wears off again!" Trampling through a flower garden, she headed directly toward what looked to be a barn.

"Looks like the horses live better than most of us do." She huffed. Yanking open the door she felt the wall for a light switch.

Mike flipped on his flashlight. "She has to be in here if you heard a scream from the bath."

"A scream?" said Andy.

"Yes from the bath," said Bert.

"My, my," said Joe.

"Shut up you two before I kick your sorry asses and make you cry in front of the cops." Kendall shot the two medics a look to kill.

"Could you at least fill us in on what we are looking for?" said Bert.

"Yeah, why would CJ play hide and seek in a barn?" said Joe.

The three others shared a look between them.

"Guys, the girls were kidnapped by two brothers who we believe have committed several murders. Kendall got away. CJ's still missing," Mike said, scanning the room for anything to point the way to CJ.

The medics looked stunned. "Well let's get going!" said Joe.

"What do you want us to do?" Bert asked.

"Let's split up and tear this place apart. These two were real sickos, so look for a special place, maybe a secret room or trap door," said Andy.

Kendall started to walk toward a door at the far end of the barn. Horses neighed and whickered to her as she passed by their stalls. "Hey!" she said as a vice grip closed around her arm.

"Oh no you don't. I've sucked face with you enough for tonight. Joe hand me a couple Narcan syringes. I'll stay with Kendall."

Kendall ignored him. "Now if I wanted a room hidden from mommy and daddy's prying eyes, where would I put it?" Reaching for the door she twisted the knob and swung it open, revealing a staircase. Bending down she picked up a silver earring. "She's here all right." She handed it to Mike. "Look. That's CJ's. "

"Give me the light Mike."

"Oh no you don't. You've been a hero enough for one day. I'm going first." Mike took the lead, never letting go of Kendall's hand. "You still OK? Need anymore?" he waved the Narcan in front of her.

"I'm fine. I think the heroin's wearing off."

Mike shone the light around the hayloft, crammed full of bales of the finest alfalfa and hay. "Doesn't this look a lot smaller than it should for the size of the first floor?"

"I was thinking the same thing. What do you think? A false wall or something?" Kendall tapped the wall next to the stairs. It sounded solid.

Together they traced the entire length of the barn, each on one side, hitting the walls with their fists.

When Kendall reached a narrow area off to the right of the loft she struck pay dirt with a hollow thud. "Mike over here. I think I've got something!"

Mike walked over, striking the wall with the maglight. "This is it." He felt around the wall. "There's got to be a door somewh-" Before him the wall slid into itself, revealing a passageway.

Mike called Andy over his portable. "Get the medics and come to the hay loft. Now!"

Shouts and footsteps sounded below, traveling up the stairs into the loft. "Over here!" Mike shouted.

Kendall slipped through the doorway. "Come on you guys!" she shouted.

Mike handed her the light. Slowly she made her way down a narrow passage way, barely wide enough for her, much less the men following behind her. Up ahead there was a gap in the wall. "I'm scared what we'll find Mike," she whispered.

"I know baby. Me too."

Together they made their way to the opening. "I'll go first," said Mike squeezing past her like two sardines in a can.

"Right behind you," said Kendall.

Andy was breathing down her back as she climbed through the opening into a large room filled with various devices of torture.

Oh, please no," she muttered.

Andy brushed past her going to Mike's side. "What the hell is this place?" He said, horror written all over his face.

Mike's light fluttered around the room, finally coming to rest on a narrow table. "Don't look Kendall," he commanded. "Bert, Joe, over here now!"

The medics raced past Kendall.

"Like hell," she shouted. Fast on Joe and Bert's heels she made her way over to the table.

Professionalism took over for the three medics. Surrounding CJ's naked body, they worked as a team to save her.

"She's barely breathing," said Joe. "Hand me the airway kit."

"Weak carotid," said Bert. "Hand me the monitor Mike," he commanded. "And find me some better light."

Kendall pumped up the blood pressure cuff. "Eighty over forty," she said mechanically. "She's lost a lot of blood. I'll start the line and give a fluid challenge."

Andy hit a light switch, revealing the atrocities CJ had suffered. Heavy metal manacles secured her arms to the table. Blood gushed from her neck where a narrow piece of wire with sharp metal points kept her from moving and bit into her flesh each time she had struggled.

"Fuckin' animals!" said Grey. Feverishly he pried at the restraints with his Swiss army knife.

"Come on CJ. We've got ya now. You can do it," said Kendall. "IV's in. Do we have an ambulance here to transport?"

Mike nodded. "The Franklin Lakes Ambulance just pulled up." Keying his portable he radioed CJ's location. "Bring a backboard, c-collar and oxygen." He also called for the state team to investigate and secure the Black estate.

Ten minutes later the paramedics and emergency medical technicians had secured CJ to the board. Mike and Andy carried her out of the barn and to the waiting ambulance.

Mike poked his head into the warm, patient compartment. "Kendall, I have to stay here until the scene is secured. I'll be at the hospital as soon as possible. You're going to Saint Joe's right?"

Kendall nodded her face pasty white.

"Joe and Bert, see that she gets checked out too."

Bert flashed him a salute while Joe eased Kendall into the captain's chair and secured her seat belt. "Time to be a patient Ms. Rose," he said.

Kendall didn't fight him. Her friend lay unconscious and intubated before her. She felt helpless. She held out her arm and examined the puncture mark in her skin. An ordeal awaited her too. What if it wasn't a clean needle he'd used to inject her?

Right now AIDS or hepatitis could be coursing through her body. Blood would be drawn as a baseline and then for the next year.

She looked up. "Mike."

He managed a weary smile. "Yes sweetheart?"

"Would you ask the cops to save any needles they find where I was? They need to be tested."

What she was saying dawned on him. "Oh honey, of course I will. Don't worry, you'll be fine." He climbed up into the rig. "Besides, no matter what happens, I'm never letting you get away from me again." He knelt beside her and kissed the puncture wound, her hand, and then her lips. "I love you Kendall. Through good or bad."

She smiled. "You're still a moronic, boob headed, pond scum, liver lily, jerk, you know."

Wrinkling his face he said, "And I look forward to you telling me that for the rest of our lives."

She rolled her eyes. "Time will tell." She turned to Bert and Joe. "You boys ready?"

The automatic vent beside her hissed, sending oxygen through the tube in CJ's lungs. She watched CJ's chest expand then deflate with each puff.

Andy sat on the bench seat holding CJ's hand, "Come on baby hold on. You can make it." He turned to Kendall, concern in his eyes. "I can't lose her now. Not when I just found her."

Kendall moved to the bench seat beside him. "She's a tough one Andy. She'll make it."

She squeezed his other hand and leaned forward to whisper in CJ's ear. "You come back to us girlfriend. Andy's the prince you've been waiting for."

Andy tensed. "I think she squeezed my hand."

"Squeeze his hand again CJ if you can hear me," said Kendall.

Weakly her hand moved again.

"CJ open your eyes. You're in an ambulance on the way to Saint Joseph's. It's Andy. Kendall, Joe, and Bert are here too."

CJ's eyes opened slowly, fear pervading them. Gagging she struggled to get up.

Kendall leaned over her. "CJ you're intubated. You have to stay calm and keep your head down until the trauma team can look at you." Smoothing CJ's bangs she smiled. "OK girlfriend?"

CJ nodded.

"Good to have you back," said Kendall. She motioned for Andy to lean forward. "And look who hasn't left your side since we found you."

CJ's lips formed a smile around the endotracheal tube. Andy kissed her forehead and cheek. "I'm not leaving you honey."

Bert and Joe nodded as Mike climbed out, shutting the side door behind him. Praying for both the girls, he silently made his way back to the barn.

Sixty-three

"Trauma team to room one, stat!" shouted the nurse over the intercom.

He carried her limp body into the room, placing her gently onto the cool metal table.

"What happened?" asked the surgeon calmly.

"Stabbing to the abdomen. I've tried to stop the bleeding, but it's seeping through the dressings." Phil pulled his bloodied hand away.

Bela moaned softly. Phil stroked her soft fur. "It's OK honey. Hang in there."

Surgeon Randi Ross lifted the dressings. "Deep cut to the left lower quadrant with heavy bleeding." She directed the surrounding trauma team. "Start two large bore IV's and give her a fluid bolus of five hundred cc's. Set up for intubation." Like a well-oiled machine the trauma team worked to save Bela's life.

The doctor took Phil aside. "She'll need immediate surgery," she said, pausing. "The cost will be considerable."

"The hell with money. I'll sign." He looked back at the heroic dog. "Just save her!"

The vet nodded. "Very well then." She patted his arm. "Do you have a phone I can reach you on?"

Phil shook his head. "I'd rather wait until I know how she is. Please just go save her."

"You'll have to give a statement to the police. I report all violent acts to the police." The doctor sternly said.

"Actually," said Phil as he opened his wallet to flash the silver badge with a golden triangle overlaid. "I am the police. That dog in there is a hero. She saved a life tonight." He touched her petite hand. "I don't want her to pay for that with her own."

Dr. Ross looked at him with new respect. "I promise I'll do everything I can Trooper Summers."

She touched his shoulder then walked briskly through the double doors into the operating room.

Phil walked to the waiting room and sat down on the green, cushioned chairs. Lowering his head he prayed silently for CJ, Kendall, and Bela.

Sixty-four

Miles away, across county, the rig pulled up in front of emergency at Saint Joseph's Hospital. Inside two trauma teams waited for CJ and Kendall.

Joe jumped out as Bert unlocked the stretcher pulling it out. Climbing down the steps, Andy held CJ's hand as she was lowered from the rig. She locked eyes with him, fighting the choking sensation of the endotracheal tube. She was weak, but alive. He squeezed her hand. "I'll never leave you again baby," he said.

Joe stayed behind with Kendall who stubbornly wanted to walk in on her own. "Easy there young lady. Stop being a bad patient and sit down until they bring out a wheelchair.

"I want to go in with CJ!" she snapped.

Joe shook his head. "Don't make me come in there!"

Tears dripped down her face as she plopped down in the seat. "Well that will do it," said Joe. He climbed into the rig, putting his arm around Kendall's shoulder. "She's going to make it."

"Did you see what they did to her? They were animals." Silent sobs racked her body.

Outside a wheelchair appeared. Easing her out of her seat he helped her down to the chair and wheeled her inside. The automatic double doors opened revealing a bustling emergency department.

"Put her in trauma two," said a nurse to Joe.

Joe wheeled her past trauma one where CJ lay on a stretcher surrounded by the trauma team. If she had a chance this was the place she'd get it. Saint Joseph's

Hospital was one of the best trauma centers in New Jersey.

Bert gave report to the head trauma surgeon as the rest of the team worked efficiently to save CJ.

Andy waved to Kendall, huddled in a corner out of the way. She smiled as she saw him shake his head when a nurse asked him to leave. He really was a good guy. CJ's handsome prince she'd been waiting for.

Would she have a chance to live the fairy tale? Kendall bowed her head as the wheelchair came to a stop beside the stretcher in trauma two. "Please save CJ," she prayed out loud.

A quick squeeze on her shoulder brought her back to the present. "Hang in there Kendall," said Joe. Kendall grabbed Joe's extended hand and pulled herself to an unsteady, standing position and then onto the waiting stretcher.

"Thanks for everything Joe. You saved my life. You, Jerry, Mike, and Bert."

Joe turned, giving her a wink as he pulled the curtain for privacy. "And don't think we're ever going to let you forget it."

The curtain slid quickly, obscuring Joe from view. Quickly the trauma team surrounded her, gently prodding her body and mind for information leading to her injuries.

Sixty-five

In trauma one CJ clung stubbornly to life as the ventilator whooshed air in and out of her lungs. Her thighs ached, burning where the flesh between them had been ripped open.

What have they done to me? Will I ever be able to be intimate with a man or have children? Tears flooded her eyes, rolling down her face. Focusing her attention on the activity around her she gauged the mood of the room. The trauma team was acting professional yet each one of them, especially the females, had a look of horror mixed with pity on their faces. Trying to speak, she fought the tube in her mouth.

"Easy CJ," cooed the trauma doctor. "We need you to remain calm so we can determine your injuries." As he petted her head the latex of his gloves caught on loose strands of hair. "I know you're scared, but you're in good hands."

"Does it hurt when I press here?" he asked, pressing down on her belly. "Blink once for yes. Twice for no."

Fluttering her eyelids she closed them once, grimacing at the hot pain shooting through her abdomen.

"Get me the gynecologist on call immediately," said the trauma surgeon.

Lower down his gloved hand came away drenched in blood. "Get me that type and cross immediately! She needs blood."

As he continued his exam the portable x-ray machine rolled into the room. The tech angled it next to the stretcher.

"Hi, CJ," she said, pulling out a portable film. "I'm going to take a few x-rays. I'll do my best not to hurt you."

Suddenly the x-ray tech shouted for the doctor to look at something. Weakness filled her body as she felt her life's blood draining from her. Moments later she floated over to Andy, admiring his handsome face staring at her body with love and concern. Reaching out she caressed his face, recoiling as her hand went through him.

Suddenly a white light shone above her, bathing her body in warmth. It was calling to her, telling her to come, that her pain would be over. Release, let go, come to me.

Rising upward she hovered beneath the stark white ceiling. Beneath, a controlled commotion surrounded her still form. She noticed the doctor looked downright scared as he shouted orders to the team. She watched as a huge needle plunged into her chest. I don't even feel it. Cool!

She floated over to the automatic vital machine and hovered in front of it watching the numbers change. Blood pressures 60 over 40. That's not good.

Oh well, she thought. She shot up turning somersaults in the air above the stretcher. The room sure was noisy with all the shouting and monitors beeping.

The light felt good, pulling her upward yet not with real strength. Wasn't she supposed to get sucked into the light where her grandma was waiting to greet her? Her excitement grew as Buttons, her childhood mutt, wagged his tail, calling for her to rub him behind the ears. He loved that. Waving her arms up and down she hoisted her body closer to them.

Suddenly she stopped flailing, warmth filling in her hand, different than the lights, deeper, growing up her arm. Glancing down one last time at her body, her eyes locked on another pair looking at her—not at her physical body, but upward at her hovering inches from the ceiling. She felt him squeeze her hand, her physical hand.

Gazing at the man she knew in her heart she loved more than heaven itself, her spirit slowly drifted down until she was once again even with Andy's face.

His eyes still locked on hers, he smiled and whispered her name. "CJ, how can you leave me when we've only just found each other?"

Below her she felt his hand squeeze hers as the white light receded. Looking up she saw the twinkling light form into a smile.

Pain washed through her body as the tube stuck in her throat made her gag. No, don't leave me, she called silently to the dimming light hovering just below the ceiling. In a blink it was gone, replaced by the face of the man who would help her through this.

Andy covered her ear with his mouth, blocking out the sound of the trauma team frantically working to stabilize her plummeting blood pressure. "Welcome back sweetheart," he said, softly.

"Blood pressure's stabilizing at 100 over 70," said a nurse.

"Excellent. Let's get her up to surgery stat," shouted the trauma surgeon.

Andy raced with the team wheeling her to the operating room. Looking down he winked at her. "Hang in there kiddo. We've got a lot of living to do."

No, it wasn't her time to go. Not with a man like this to live for. They lifted her body onto the operating table as a nurse injected something into an IV port. "Sweet dreams," she said to CJ. "You'll be good as new in a few hours."

With that, blackness filled her view and she let herself fall into a dreamless sleep.

Sixty-six

Kendall watched with horror as CJ was rushed past her to the operating room. She hadn't missed a thing that had gone on next to her despite the curtains that separated rooms one and two. "Hang in there, girl," she called. Andy waved back. "You too, Kendall," he called.

"Need a warm blanket honey?" asked a nurse.

Kendall nodded, shivering in the thin gown. But it wasn't the cold that made her shake. It was plain, cold, fear. Fear for CJ. Fear for what awaited her.

A lab tech popped into the room with bright, bouncy steps. Setting down his tray he checked the band around Kendall's wrist. "My name's Alan and I'll be drawing your blood."

He looked about twelve years old. "You old enough to use that thing?" asked Kendall, eyeing the needle in his hand.

"Sure thing," he said confidentially, taking no offense.

"Must get that a lot, huh?" said Kendall.

He nodded, smiling as he plunged the needle into her arm. "See? Got it first shot." He drew several tubes before pulling out the needle and applying pressure to the site with a gauze pad. "You'll need to sign paperwork authorizing the AIDS test. I'll be right back with it."

She nodded, fearful of sending the blood. Once in the lab she couldn't get it back. Couldn't stop the reality of what the results might bring to her life.

The vampire boy came back into the room with a slip. "So you're a medic?" he asked.

"Fifteen years," she said.

"Then you know that the chance of you contracting AIDS from a needle stick is very low."

"Yeah, I know. But it doesn't make this any easier."

He nodded. "If it helps, I've been stuck three times now and one was a confirmed AIDS patient." He held out a pen for her to sign the form he'd placed in front of her. "It's been two years since then and I've tested negative."

"Even if I don't get AIDS, there's still Hepatitis B and C," she said, shuddering.

"I'm negative for those too," he said, squeezing her hand. "So don't panic. Ok!"

"Thanks. I really appreciate you sharing this with me. It makes me feel a little better."

He made a silly face. "Only a little better?"

She smiled for the first time that night. "Alright, a lot better."

"Well detective, I guess I best be getting back to blood sucking."

"Detective?" she said.

The tech nodded. "I've never seen so many cops, troopers, and medics crammed into one waiting room. They're jamming the whole parking lot with medic trucks and cruisers.

Hell the way the night's going, I'm sure the fire trucks will be arriving any minute. Word is you and your partner are some kind of super sleuths who tracked down a serial killer."

"In that case, you mind getting this super sleuth another heated blanket? I'm freezing."

The tech nodded. "Ah, I think someone's here to see you."

The curtain opened revealing the ultimate, Marlboro man, minus the smokes. His trooper uniform looked battered and dirty. He stood there, nervously fingering his hat.

"Hey there handsome," she said, holding out her arms.

His muscled body enveloped her in the warmest bear hug she'd ever felt.

"How are you?" he whispered anxiously. Cradling her to his chest her sobs shook his body. "Ah, baby. I'm here. It's gonna be OK."

Wiping tears from her blue eyes she whispered, "I love you Mike."

Sitting bolt upright he gently extricated her body from his. "Say that again." Hope filled his face. Hope for forgiveness and the future.

Kendall looked up at the man she'd never been able to shake from her system. "I said I love you, you bit dopey-looking cluck."

"Flattery will get you everywhere Ms. Rose." He kissed her lightly at first then deeply as his pent up love came flooding out.

"Hey, get a room you two!" called Joe from the nurse's station.

A startled Kendall and Mike parted as a round of applause began to build, softly at first then with a loud crescendo. Mike stood up bowing at the gathering crowd. "Thank you and good night," he said, pulling the curtain shut with a chuckle.

"Guess you won't need this?" said Alan, waving the blanket through a small slit in the curtain.

Kendall smiled, throwing a pillow squarely in his chest.

"Nope, guess not," he said, amidst laughter.

Sixty-seven

Two weeks later.

Seven pm.

Tears streaming down her face, she knelt by the dark casket, placing her hand on the shiny wood. It seemed surreal looking at this box holding the body of her friend. The room was crowded with people remembering a person so vibrant and loved.

Kneeling on the velvet step, she reflected on the events leading up to this depressing day. Why did this have to happen? She didn't believe a word of what was being said about her friend and she never would. Loyalty was a trait she held in high regard and one she demanded back from anyone close to her.

A strong hand rubbed her back. She looked over at Mike kneeling next to her, his long legs stretched out behind him. She thanked God for sending him back into her life. Tragedies like this made one realize what's really valuable in life. Not things, not holding on to grudges or old hurts. Love that was what was important. Giving and receiving love.

Mike placed his large hand over top of hers. "I'm so sorry honey."

"I know," she whispered, tears threatening to fall once more.

The room hushed in silence behind them. They turned to see what was going on. Surprise registered on the crowd's face as Bob Crosby's estranged family—father, mother, brother, and sister entered warily. Bob had been well respected and loved by many. Everyone knew something bad had estranged his parents from him. Kendall knew they hadn't spoken to Bob in over ten years. Ten wasted years.

Kendall and Mike stood up, waiting as the four made their way single file to the casket. "They came," said Kendall.

How she wanted to lash out, to tell them what fools they'd been to miss out on knowing their son. Luckily for them she respected Bob enough to keep her mouth shut.

The family eyed the two people standing by the casket with daggers in their eyes. Mrs. Crosby had obviously been crying, her eyes red and her nose running. She dabbed her face with a dainty white handkerchief as she stood apart from her husband who extended his hand.

"You must be Kendall," he said.

She nodded, not reciprocating.

His hand fell back to his side. He sighed wearily.

"Your son was a wonderful man and my good friend," said Kendall.

Mrs. Crosby brushed past her husband of thirty-five years. Taking Kendall's hands in hers she bowed her head slightly. "I've been a fool," she cried. Tears streamed down her pale face as she looked up at Kendall.

"I'd have to agree with you there, Mrs. Crosby." She blinked tears away. "Bob told me you hadn't spoken to him in over ten years, but until his murder I never knew why."

Pulling her hands from Mrs. Crosby's grasp, she stepped back turning to Mike.

Mike cleared his throat. "From every piece of evidence I gathered your son was innocent of all charges."

Mrs. Crosby nodded. "He was proven innocent. But that was never good enough for my husband!"

Mr. Crosby's shaking hand reached out to touch his wife. She pulled back. "You see the girl's father was an important client of mine. He won't let it drop." Rubbing his cold hands together he turned to his wife. "For the sake of our family, we had to distance ourselves from Bob."

"You mean you did, and along with that you forced us to disown him too," she spat.

The room grew quiet as Bob's friends listened to the argument. "Mrs. Crosby, this isn't the time for this," said Kendall softly, glancing at the closed coffin.

"Oh I think it is. I listened to Matt for too long. I didn't want to displease you dear husband, and because of my weakness our dear son died without knowing how much I loved him. I can't forgive myself or you for that."

"He knew," said Bob's brother Art.

"How can you say that?" said Mrs. Crosby.

Her daughter Cindy came to her, putting her arm around her mother's waist. "Because not everyone listened to dad." She smiled sadly, taking her brother's hand in hers. "We've kept in close touch with Bob for the past few years."

Art reached out and squeezed his mother's hand. "Bob knew, because we told him every time we saw him."

"You saw him!" said Mr. Crosby, relief coursing through his strained voice.

Art nodded, pulling his father into the family circle. "Not everyone's as scared of you as mom."

Momentarily, a smile crossed his face. "Thank you both for not listening to me."

"Well I'll be damned," said Kendall. Mike pulled her sleeve edging them away from the embracing family.

Outside the room Kendall leaned against the pasty wallpaper. "No matter how hard I try I can't forget how Bob died. The terror and guilt he must have felt forced by Tommy to..."

Mike pulled her into his strong embrace. "Shush honey. Bob wouldn't want to be remembered in this way. He was a free, funny spirit."

She sniffled, hugging him closer. "You're right." She looked up startled when Mike began to cry. "Honey what's wrong?"

"If it wasn't for Bob I could have lost you forever." He kissed the top of her head. "I can't imagine the courage it took to plant those clues with that bastard holding a gun to his head."

Kendall nodded. "He always did want to be the author of a murder mystery."

"I guess in his own way he was, wasn't he?" said Mike.

"I wish Bob were here to see this, to know about his family."

Mike looked upward. "Knowing Bob, I'm sure he is sweetheart."

The grandfather clock began to sound. "Shall we," said Kendall

Hand in hand they left the funeral home. There was still time to visit CJ before visiting hours were over. Not that visiting hours mattered to a medic and state trooper. Their jobs pretty much let them visit anytime. CJ's assigned nurse, however, wasn't impressed. Together they ran to Mike's 'Vette.

Sixty-eight

CJ sat in the hospital bed, propped up by thick, white pillows. The room looked sterile except for the few cards and flowers allowed in intensive care. Tubes ran into CJ's veins delivering life-saving drugs from the suspended plastic bags.

"Hi there kiddo," said Mike, brightly.

CJ smiled at the handsome man she once called a Marlboro man, minus the smokes. "Hi there yourself."

Kendall rushed to the bed, leaning over the side rail to give her friend a quick hug. "Where did your man go? The guy hasn't left your side in days."

"My man," she said dreamily.

"Is?" said Mike.

"He is taking a break in the café. He so enjoys the hospital food, I don't know how I'm going to get him to leave once I'm better."

"I'll offer him a home-cooked meal," said Kendall.

Mike and CJ shot each other looks.

"Yeah that will do it," said Mike, sarcastically. Kendall started to stomp over. "I think I'll go join Andy and give you two women some time alone," said Mike as he scurried out of Kendall's reach.

"You're a dork," quipped Kendall at his retreating back. The door swung closed and she turned back to CJ. "So girlfriend, how are you?"

"I don't know. Sometimes I forget and feel like it was all a dream. Then suddenly I'm back on that table being tortured by them."

Kendall climbed onto the bed next to CJ, taking care not to pull out the IV. "Oh honey. I'm so sorry."

CJ squeezed her hand. "I've never gotten a chance to thank you for saving my life."

Kendall hugged friend. "Did you really think I'd let you cut out on me brat?"

CJ laughed. "You'd never let me get off that easy. Not you!"

"I'm so glad we're friends again." She sighed. "I've really missed you CJ."

"Me too." CJ brushed her face against Kendall's sleeve.

"Yo, missy, did you just use my sleeve as a snot rag?"

CJ snorted. "Graduated number one from charm school."

Kendall laughed, brushing away an imaginary goober off her shirt. "Seriously CJ, how are you handling what happened. Did you call May like I told you?"

"You mean your little rent-a-friend?" CJ's smile brightened. "I did. I think she's really going to help me. She's been here every day and once I'm released I'll be able to go see her in her office."

Kendall nodded. "Good. She helped me get through my parents' death among many things. I wouldn't be the person I am today if it wasn't for her help." Kendall leaned back. "She's going to help you work through this honey. I know it."

"Andy's being so patient too," she sniffled. "Who'd have thought I'd meet my soul mate in your kitchen. I mean seeing as how for humanity's sake, not to mention my stomach, it's hardly ever used."

Kendall punched her in the arm. "Very funny, and I was serious about the home-cooked dinner too." Kendall ruffled the brunette's hair. "I'm happy to see your sense of humor, little though there is, is still intact."

CJ turned to her, serious written all over her face. "Kendall?"

"What CJ?"

"I'm scared."

Lacing her fingers through CJ's hand she said, "I know you are. Do you want to talk about it?"

CJ's teeth started to chatter and tears began dripping down her face onto her trembling body. "Will I ever be normal again?"

"Of course you will. As normal as anyone who's a paramedic can be." Kendall squeezed her hand, smiling. "That's a joke. Laugh anytime you feel like it."

"I don't mean emotionally. I mean, you know, physically." Silent cries racked her body. "After what they did to me."

She exhaled a whoosh of air she'd been holding in. "Didn't the doctor tell you?"

CJ shook her head. "If she did, I was too out of it to remember."

"Well then the answer to your question is yes!"

"How do you know for sure?"

"Honey, that woman couldn't wait to get away from me when I was done grilling her yesterday. I figured you wouldn't remember everything so I made her go over every detail with me." Kendall rubbed the back of her tense neck. "All the damage those bastards did to you was repaired in surgery."

Hope lit up CJ's face. "All of it?"

Kendall shook her head yes. "Girlfriend you're gonna be sore as hell for a few months but once you're healed," she paused, smiling.

"What?" said CJ, frowning.

"Frankly my dear, it's not you I'm worried about," said Kendall as the door swung open. She motioned her head, giggling as Andy and Mike strolled in, ice cream cones in hand. "Hope that boy takes vitamins, cause once you're ready to ride the pony he's not gonna know what hit him."

CJ pinched Kendall's thigh. "Ha, shark-bite,"

Kendall yelped. "Hey woman, you don't use that secret weapon on another woman." She jerked her finger toward the guys. "That's for man control only."

CJ giggled, taking her chocolate cone from Andy.

Kendall patted her space on the bed. "Come here trigger. You can have my spot."

Andy ambled over looking between the beaming faces of CJ and Kendall. "Trigger?" he said suspiciously, plopping down on the bed. "Just what have you two ladies been talking about?"

CJ looked at Kendall with a smirk covering her lips. "Ladies?"

"Oh honey," said Kendall smartly. "We never said we wuz ladies."

The two men looked at each other, rolling their eyes.

"Mike, just what have I gotten myself into?" said Andy.

Mike pulled Kendall into him. "Andy my man, some things are better left unsaid." He held out his hand.

Andy gripped it tightly.

"Welcome to the he-man hell-cat lovers club. One thing I can promise you is you'll never be bored."

The foursome smiled, enjoying the ice cream and each other's company until a grinning Nurse Ratchet kicked them out at ten.

Sixty-nine

She parked the Firebird outside the cabin rented under the alias of Sybil Windslow. They picked Walpack for its low population, something like 35 people, and for its isolation. Were they really going through with this? Sure the guy was a confirmed cheater, that hadn't been hard to figure out. But wow, this was gonna pay him back in spades! He deserved it, she reasoned, taking off her long coat and hanging it in the foyer closet.

Don't think she hadn't wanted to do this to Mike when he cheated on her. The difference was she only fantasized, not acted.

Glancing at the kitchen clock, she quickly picked up the bags she brought and carried them into the main bedroom. She'd planned on more time to set up but arrived late, not realizing just how far away Walpack was from civilization. Thirty minutes to go before Bobbie arrived with the unsuspecting, cheating husband of hers.

She looked in the mirror and removed the short brunette wig and brushed out her long, feathered blonde hair. Removing the oversized man's shirt and shorts, she walked over to the full-length mirror.

Adjusting the leather straps on the bodice, she pulled the thirty-four, b-cups together showing off her cleavage.

Bending down she pulled off her sneakers and socks, then slid on thigh-high patent leather boots with stiletto heels. She zipped them up, stood tall and studied herself in the mirror. "Not bad for an old broad," she said, smiling. Heck, maybe they could pull this off.

She'd be dead if Mike ever found out. How would he though, being stationed at the Totowa Barracks. Word would travel fast, but not so fast that she couldn't be home in time to make him his favorite supper.

She wished Bobbie could let go and give it time like she had. Still, no matter, what she'd support her friend.

It took the whole half hour to arrange the lit candles around the room, along with a host of other surprises.

Outside she heard a car coming up the drive. Pulling back the curtain, she saw a red head behind the wheel with Chris sitting beside her in the passenger seat. The big dope had such an expectant, excited look on his face she started to giggle. He has no idea what awaits him, she thought, as she poured three glasses of champagne and listened to the front door creak open.

"Baby I've dreamed of having you and Kendall since the day I met her. I can't believe you're doing this for me," said Chris, his voice full of excitement.

Bobbie smiled, leading Chris into the room where Kendall waited holding a whip.

"Take off your clothes and lay down on the bed now!" ordered Kendall.

Chris shivered with excitement, reaching out to fondle Kendall's breast.

She slapped it away with a flick of the crop whip. "Not until I say you can. Now do as I say or I'm leaving."

Obediently Chris stripped and lay down on the stiff bed.

Kendall smiled, leaning across his bare chest. Quickly she slapped a handcuff around his wrist and secured it to a bolt ring in the wall. Bobbie did the same on the other side.

"Oh honey, you won't believe the fun we have in store for you," cooed Bobbie.

Across the room Kendall smiled as she pulled on jeans over her bodice.

"What's going on?" said Chris, yanking against the handcuffs. "This isn't funny. Let me out!"

"Don't worry honey. Help will be on the way shortly," said Bobbie. She buttoned her high-collar shirt and took out a marker. "Good thing you never did have a hairy chest," she said, beginning to write. "Give my regards to your new partner." She spat on his face.

Fear crossed his face, his eyes darting back and forth between Kendall and Bobbie. "What are you two doing to me?"

"Don't worry Chris, help will be on the way shortly," said Kendall sarcastically. She picked up her purse and checked the room for any trace that they had been there. "Coming Bobbie?"

Bobbie smiled, adding the finishing touch to her soon-to-be ex-husband's chest. "Give my regards to your rescuers." Pointing her finger like a gun she fired, following Kendall out the door.

The brunette and the red head drove away in separate cars. The brunette had one more stop to make at a local pay phone. Angling the Firebird next to the auto friendly phone, she dialed the inside line for the Sussex county state police barracks.

No it wasn't an emergency, but did require a police response. No she didn't want to give her name or get involved, but she'd been walking by a cabin and heard a man yelling for help. Yes, she'd looked in the window, but the doors are all locked. Yes, please send out a rescue team as the man's handcuffed naked to the bed and keeps screaming for help.

Seventy

Passaic County Jail.

July 5th

The Passaic County Jail sat on Main Street in downtown Paterson. Parking was a pain in the butt on a good day. Luckily she'd been able to borrow the paramedic supervisor's vehicle. Actually she wasn't really borrowing the suburban; it came with her new job— Clinical Coordinator for the Wayne General Paramedic Unit.

She'd been in this position for the past three months, responsible for training and recertification of the paramedics and emergency medical technicians. She hadn't given up the street though, and was regularly scheduled to ride the truck at least once a week.

Pulling into the lot, she stopped by a narrow building. Inside a Passaic County sheriff's officer pushed open the window.

"Hi, can I park this somewhere? I'm here to see a prisoner."

"Sure thing." He pointed to a space between the HazMat vehicle and a patrol car. "Just take that space there."

"Thanks! I appreciate it." She parked and then lowered the mirror to freshen her makeup and hair. She wore her dark navy uniform to help ease the security procedures.

Walking inside she picked up the phone to the guard desk. "Hi, I'm here to see a prisoner."

Through the bulletproof window he waved her over to the side where a corrections officer stood beside a metal detector. He handed her a sign-in log. "Sign there. Who are you here to see?"

"Black," she said.

"Ah, the infamous Mr. Black. What a weirdo he is. Hasn't stopped crying about his brother since he got here. Deserves what he gets, that one."

Kendall nodded, passing through the metal detector, which set off a series of loud beeps.

"Better remove the radio and jewelry Miss."

Taking off her earrings, she set them on the table along with her keys, belt, and portable radio.

"Don't forget the badge," said the guard.

"So much for easing the security check," she mumbled. Unclasping the gold badge, she placed it next to the rest of the items and walked through the now quiet metal detector.

"Clear to go," said the guard. Handing her the items from the table he added, "Be careful."

She secured the belt around her waist and put the jewelry and badge in her pocket. "Thanks. I will."

"Follow officer Peters. He'll take you to Black."

Black was being held in solitary confinement. The guard deposited her in a large room filled with several tables and chairs.

Several minutes later the door at the end of the room opened. Surrounded by two large guards and shackled by the wrists and ankles stood Johnnie Black. His green eyes lit up as they lay upon Kendall. He gingerly maneuvered across the room to where she sat.

"Hello Kendall," he said softly. "Thank you for coming."

"Hi, Johnnie," she said. Turning to the guards she pointed to the shackles. "Can he be released while we talk?"

One of the guards standing over six foot five spoke. "No ma'am. I'm sorry, but for security reasons he must remain shackled."

Kendall nodded, waiting for Johnnie to ease himself into a plastic chair. They sat facing each other in silence.

"Why did you want to see me Johnnie?" Kendall said, breaking the silence.

He flashed his perfect white teeth. "Do you miss me?"

"Johnnie, please," she said, exasperated. Taking out a notebook she flipped open a blank page. "What is it you want?"

His green eyes blazed. "You." Black leaned back in the chair, his chains rattling against the metal legs. His arms and chest were enormous, proof of what he'd been doing with his free time.

She scratched her nose nervously. He could crush her neck with one squeeze. Shuffling her feet she moved her chair away from the table.

"So?" said Johnnie. Leaning across the table he placed his cuffed hands in front of Kendall.

"So nothing." Narrowing her eyes she said, angrily, "You know it wasn't even your baby, it was Jack's. He loved her and was going to marry her." She shook her head. "All the killing for what?"

"Why do you have to bring that up? I read the report." His face contorted inches from hers. "I'm glad I made the bastard's father's life miserable like mine."

"What are you talking about?" she said softly. Reaching out she touched his cuffed hands. "There's nothing wrong with Jack. I saw him on a call yesterday."

Johnnie leaned back, smiling sickly. "Yeah, but now Jackie poo doesn't have his rich daddy to go to. Does he?"

"Doctor Garrison died of a hypertensive crisis."

"Did he?" Black laughed sarcastically. "What do you think was really happening while you waited and waited for 911 to pick up?"

"You handcuffed him."

"Is that all I did Kendall?" His face tilted up to the ceiling. "You people are all so stupid."

"Oh are we really?" she said angrily.

"I mean you didn't even spot it."

"What are you talking about?" She tapped her fingers on the table. Johnnie leaned closer toward her. "Garrison knew too much that night he came to your house. He was so close to figuring it out, and we couldn't let him do that now could we?"

"Spot what you lunatic? There wasn't a mark on him other than the place where you put the handcuffs."

He giggled, pushing himself away from the table. "You really should have taken a closer look. Maybe you would have caught me right there. But no you take it at face value. Foolish girl."

Scratching her neck she went to rise. "I've had enough of your games. Good luck to you Johnnie. You'll need it!"

"Isuprel," he said, smartly.

"What about it?" Turning, she walked toward the door.

"Wait!" Johnnie stood so quickly the chair flipped back, crashing to the floor.

The guards jumped on Johnnie. "I suggest you sit your ass back down in that chair now Black!" said the tall, dark-skinned guard. "Are you all right Miss?"

Kendall nodded, turning back toward the prisoner. "It's OK officer." She walked back and sat down, pushing her chair away from the table.

Black seated himself, pulling himself closer to the table. "Thank you,"

"Tell me what you are talking about now or I swear I'm out of here," she said.

"What the hell; I'm already going down," He paused, staring her down. "Did you know Tommy was a doctor?"

"Doctor?"

"Yes until the assholes at the hospital turned him in for stealing useless drugs."

"Useless huh?" she said. "What kind of drugs? Maybe a little Morphine or Demerol?"

He shook his head wildly. "No, nothing like that," Leaning in he motioned her to come closer. Sensing her distrust, he lowered his cuffed hands under the table.

Caught in the moment, she edged closer to listen.

"Ever hear of Isuprel?"

"Of course I have. We used that when I first started as a medic. But it's long since gone out of style. Too much of a punch to a patient's heart."

"Ever wonder what it would do to a person injected directly into their brainstem?" Flashing his perfect smile he continued. "Just mix it with a little glucose then angle a needle upward and it pops right through the base of the skull into the brain. The ventricles suck it right up and whoops up his blood pressure and pulse." Strangling back a giggle, Johnnie continued; "I thought his eyes were going to bulge right out of his head. He even asked me why. Isn't that precious?"

She jerked back in her chair with a look of knowledge across her face. "Son of a bitch you killed him!"

"Was it really me?" he said with a question in his voice. "Or was it Tommy you were with?" The suppressed giggle escaped his lips. "We really are identical you know."

"You mean were, you sick bastard," she snapped back with a smirk on her face.

"Don't talk about Tommy that way!" he screamed.

The guards moved in circling the duo. "Put your hands down Black. Now!" They ordered him up against the cement wall.

Black jumped up, pounding the table with his fists. "After all you've done I still want you!"

Quickly the guards wrestled Johnnie to the ground. Kendall jumped up from the seat backing against the wall. The guards yanked Johnnie to his feet, dragging him to the door. He stuck out his feet and bound hands, refusing to be pushed through the door. Turning around a strange gleam filled his eyes. "Kendall remember this—I'm coming for you. You can count on it."

Fear and shock filled her body. "Are you threatening me Johnnie?"

The guards wrestled him onto the floor. Kicking and biting he broke free from them, heading right for Kendall. From the side door several more guards ran in, an alarm blaring overhead. One of them ran head first into Johnnie tackling him to the ground. The rest piled on top of him, punching and screaming obscenities.

Kendall watched in horror. From the mass of bodies she heard him scream her name. A female guard took her by the arm leading her out the door.

As she left the room she heard Johnnie yell. "You're mine Kendall. You'll always be mine!"

Swinging the door shut, the female guard looked at her with concern. "Are you all right Miss?"

"Did you hear him? He said he was coming for me." Kendall shuddered.

"Miss, there is no way he's getting out of here. He's watched twenty-four hours a day in solitary confinement."

Kendall shook her head willing her body to calm. "You don't know him. He's going to escape."

"I promise you he will not escape. I'll make sure everyone is on high alert." The guard handed her a glass of water from the cooler. "Here, drink this honey. You'll be OK."

Kendall took a sip then set it down on the desk. The noise had stopped from the room. "Is he gone?" she asked the guard.

"Yes. It is safe for you to leave now." She held the door open for Kendall. "I'll walk you down."

The guard at the exit area downstairs said good bye, reassuring her once again of her safety. She didn't believe her for one minute. Crazy with money was a dangerous combination. He was coming for her and she didn't doubt it for one minute.

Walking through the metal detector, she collected her things on the other side. She'd been stupid to come here and boy was Mike going to kill her when he found out. That is if Johnnie didn't beat him to it first.

What had she hoped to gain? He was a killer and a liar. She wanted to ask him about the needle Tommy used to shoot her up with. Even though it had tested negative for disease, she still worried with paranoia if it was a dirty needle. She wanted reassurance from Johnnie, but instead he had nearly crushed her.

Outside she unlocked the medic unit and got in behind the wheel. She didn't bother to fix her makeup. In nine months she'd know for certain if she'd contracted any disease. She'd just have to wait. Damn, why had she come and stirred him up. He was coming. She felt it. She knew it!

Seventy-one

February 2nd

A heavy snow fell as the call she'd been dreading woke her from a deep sleep just past midnight.

She fumbled for the phone, knocking the receiver to the floor in her drunk-like state. Reaching down, she grabbed it and gruffly answered. "Hello."

"Kendall Rose?" said a male voice.

"Speaking."

"This is Officer Kern from the Passaic County Jail."

Sitting bolt up and now wide awake, she held her breath waiting for him to utter the words she didn't want to hear.

"I'm afraid I have some news regarding Johnnie Black."

"He's escaped, hasn't he?" she said, cutting him off.

"Yes Miss, he has. It happened a little past ten tonight."

"Ten! That's two hours ago and you call me now?"

"Warwick police have been notified and they are on the way to your home as we speak, so calm down. There is nothing to worry about."

"I knew it. I told you people the day he threatened me he'd get out. But no, you all treated me like I was a crazy woman. Happy now?"

"Miss, I'm very sorry this has happened and we are doing everything we can to find him."

Slamming down the phone, she yanked open the drawer to the bedside table. She grabbed the Glock and opened it to make sure it had a full load. "Son of a bitch," she muttered.

Bela inched across the bed laying her head on Kendall's lap.

"What are we going to do girl?" she said, petting the dog's soft head.

The phone rang loudly propelling her to her feet. "Get a grip Kendall."

"Hello, who is this?" she demanded into the headset.

"Kendall, it's Mike, Calm down honey."

"Mike, he's out!"

"I know. I'm in a troop car coming to you now. Are all the doors locked?"

"Yes, but that's not going to stop him. You should have seen the size of him from working out in the prison gym. He's pumped up and crazy. Only a bullet is going to put an end to this. Let's hope my aim's fatal this time around."

"Stay in your room. That's an order. I'll be there in a few minutes."

Beside her, Bela growled. Warily she sniffed the air, staring at the door, her low growling growing louder. Sniffing the base of the door she yelped and backed away, racing to Kendall's side.

"I have to go Mike. He's right outside my door." Dropping the phone she angled the Glock in front of her body, backing against the wall. "Come on you son of a bitch. Let me finish you off this time. I'll blow your f-ing head off if you set one foot in this room."

The doorknob twisted back and forth.

She heard sirens in the distance, too far away to do her any good. A flash of movement outside her window caught her eye. He was on the roof!

A smile with perfect white teeth filled the windowpane. His fist crashed through the thick glass. "Miss me sweetheart?" he said, dripping blood onto her carpet.

Pointing the Glock she fired rapidly. The remaining glass shattered sending sharp, bloody icicles flying through the air like shrapnel.

Dropping to the floor she called Bela to her side. Like a disco ball blue and red strobe light bounced off the wall of her room as Warwick PD roared up the driveway.

Aiming the Glock in front of her, she stood slowly and walked to the open window. Carefully she glanced out. The roof was empty and she could see where someone had slipped backward. Boot prints scattered about the icy roof ending at the gutter. She hadn't missed this time!

Leaning further out the window she tried to find his crushed body lying in the snow beneath the house. "No!"

Hands shot down from above her, grabbing her hair. "See I knew you still loved me," he said, pulling her half out the window, his face inches from hers. "Now how are you going to get out of this one bitch?" he snarled.

Locking eyes with him she smiled then bit his nose. His hands let go of her hair and she fell back inside. Shots rang out from the ground below. Cops shouted, sirens wailed, help had arrived at last.

Inching her way over to where Bela lay on the floor, she comforted the scared dog. "It's OK he's gone for good now."

The dog whined softly, looking at the bedroom door. Picking up on Bela's mood, Kendall angled the gun once more out in front and walked to the door.

She unlocked the knob, twisted it and yanked open the door, jumping into the hallway ready to fire. It was clear.

Bela huffed, following a scent down the hall through the kitchen. She pawed at the door until Kendall opened it for her. Bela hurried down the stairs whining loudly with Kendall behind her ready with the Glock.

Outside Tom's door Bela stopped, her eyes filled with doggie worry. She looked up at Kendall, who quickly pushed open the unlocked door. "Tom?" she called loudly.

Bela shot past her, flying through the doorway into the murky darkness of Tom's apartment. "Bela, no!" shouted Kendall.

"Bela come here!" Kendall shouted, cautiously entering the apartment. Feeling for the wall switch she flipped it on illuminating the neat kitchen. "Tom are you here?" she called again.

Bela growled deeply from inside the living room. Racing to the aid of her canine friend she turned the corner into the dark living room tripping on the rug. Wildly her arms reached out, searching for something to stop her fall. Crashing forward, her body struck a cold form swinging from the ceiling. It moved easily to the side and she landed with a thud onto the rug.

Rolling to her side she looked up, straining to see what she'd hit. A single beam of light flashed into the room from a cop standing inside the kitchen. A piercing scream filled the air, coming from her very lips as her eyes looked into her friend's contorted face.

She jumped up, meeting the cop by Tom's body. Together they struggled to free the noose from Tom's neck. Two more cops rushed in, one with a knife to cut the rope. As a group they lowered Tom's limp form to the ground.

"Tom!" Kendall said. Opening his airway with a jaw thrust, carefully maintaining control of his spine, she pinched his nose and gave him to rescue breaths into his mouth.

One of the cops felt for a pulse. "No pulse, starting CPR."

"Kendall!" called Mike.

"In here," she yelled back, between rescue breathing. "Get your oxygen and first aid kit!"

Mike raced into the room. "What the hell happened?"

"We found Tom hanging. They killed him Mike! He's like my brother. Please save him God!"

Mike knelt down beside Tom's body and checked for a pulse. Gently he touched Kendall's shoulder. "Honey, he's not here anymore. He's gone. You have to stop CPR. Do you want him on a vent with the only thing still going in his body is his heart?"

Kendall sat back on her heels, looking down at her dear friend. "Your right. Tom would never want to be a vegetable in a nursing home." Tears fell from her face, dripping onto her pajama bottoms. "Tommy," she said, softly.

Mike fell to his knees, pulling Kendall into his broad chest. "I'm so sorry honey. Tom was a great guy."

"I can't take it Mike. First Bob and Maxie. Now Tom," she said between sobs.

"We'll get him Kendall. I swear to you we will."

Two more Warwick cops ran breathless into the room.

"Whoever did this is long gone," said the older one.

"We know who it is," said Mike, helping Kendall to her feet. "Put out an APB on Johnnie Black."

Kendall buried her head in Mike's chest. "There were two of them."

"What?" said Mike, pulling her chin up gently with his hand.

"I heard a man laughing outside my bedroom door seconds before I saw Johnnie outside the window. He can't be two places at once."

Mike exhaled. "So he has help."

Taking Kendall's hand he led her back upstairs to her apartment. "Pack some things for you and Bela. You are both staying with me until we find Black and his little friend, and end this once and for all."

Tom was buried the following week under a sunny sky. Johnnie Black still on the loose hung like a heavy fog over the crowd of Tom's grieving friends and family.

Tom had often told Kendall he wanted people to celebrate his life when he died, not mourn and cry. So in honor of his wishes they did. Celebrating his life with stories, good company, and food. Tom wouldn't be forgotten for his love lived on.

Seventy-two

April 25th

One year post heroin injection, with five negative AIDS tests and a few negative hepatitis tests behind her, Kendall stood at the altar next to her best friend CJ.

Mike smiled at her sweetly. Andy nodded, wobbling back and forth on nervous legs. White was definitely not her best color. Wiping sweat beads from her brow, she wished for a place to sit down. The minister was mumbling something she couldn't understand. She looked to Mike for some help. He smiled sweetly. She vowed never to do this again. After all, there was nothing wrong with living together in this day and age was there?

Churches made her nervous. White gowns made her nervous. Mike made her nervous. A flash of gold caught her eye as in slow motion the object moved closer and closer to its intended target. She was shaking now. Stretching out her trembling hand, she waited for the cold steel of CJ's bridal bouquet holder to touch her.

Grasping the flowers, she sighed with relief as the gold ring slipped on her friend's finger and the preacher pronounced them husband and wife.

The bride and groom kissed then took off down the aisle, followed by Kendall and Mike.

Mike shook his head, smiling at the girl beside him. He asked and asked and asked. Once on bended knee, once at the PBA Christmas party, and his most recent attempt on the S.S. Norway cruising the Caribbean. Each time she broke out in a cold sweat, mumbled her apologies, and then ran for the hills. There weren't so many hills on the S.S. Norway.

She shot him a look that said, "Oh no you don't. Not again."

Seeing him smile a smile that was definitely not sweet this time, she took off running down the steps to the waiting limo.

He looked at his watch. What the heck; they had a few minutes before the reception. He opened the door and slid in beside her.

Tapping the partition between them and the driver, Mike said, "Once around the park my good man."

Taking Kendall in his arms he kissed her passionately. "So Ms. Rose will you..."

Behind the driver's wheel the handsome, dirty blonde-haired limo driver rubbed the sore spot in his chest. The damn wound had never healed right.

Seventy-three

Smiling with perfect white teeth the driver mumbled. "Once around the park and then some my good man." Hitting the special power locks he lowered the window divider, startling the embracing couple with a loaded gun. "Hello again Kendall." A menacing frown crossed his face. "Did you really think I'd let you have her Mike?"

Mike stared back into the green eyes filled with rage. "You know," he said leaning forward. "You really should have dyed your hair a darker color. It would be so much more becoming with your eyes."

Black's face contorted with rage. "I'm going to enjoy killing you Garcia." He aimed the gun with his finger poised over the trigger. "Say good-bye Mi"

Kendall's door shot open. Bobbie Angel grabbed her body and yanked her out of the car onto the pavement. On the opposite side Trooper Hampton, due to retire within a month, wrestled Mike to the ground.

Inside the limo the bulletproof partition shot up, controlled remotely by rookie Trooper Connell.

Bullets sprayed the car, shattering the windows. Johnnie Black gurgled, blood bubbling from his lungs. He looked at Kendall, pleading with his eyes for her to help him. In the front seat Johnnie slumped over the wheel, his body sounding the horn in an eerie wail.

Mike, Dave, Bobbie, and Kendall were ushered through a crowd of onlookers and police. Medics with the swat team guided them into a waiting rig.

Mike wiped away blood from his right temple. "Lucky for me he was a poor shot."

Kendall sat next to him on the bench seat wrapping her arms around his strong body. "So much for the perfect plan. I could kill you for going along with it." Kissing him softly, she said. "Let me take a look at that."

"It's just a flesh wound." Mike smiled, doing his best Monty Python imitation. Taking her in his arms, he kissed her passionately. "You never answered my question," he said, emotionally. Shaking, he brushed back a stray blonde hair from her face.

"What question was that Trooper Garcia?"

"The same one I've asked you for the past six months."

He got down on one knee, wedging his muscular legs and torso between the stretcher and bench seat. Outside the medic smiled. "Don't be a dope this time Kendall," said Bert.

"Come on, let's give the two love birds some privacy." Joe stepped down and shut the back double doors to the ambulance.

Inside Mike pulled out a sparkling square diamond. "Kendall, will you please marry me?"

Trembling, she held out her left hand forcing herself to stay calm. Looking into Mike's blue eyes she said, "I thought you'd never ask. Yes, I'll marry you!"

Pulling her into his arms he kissed her deeply. "Yee ha!" shouted Mike.

The back doors to the rig burst open revealing a small crowd. "She finally said yes!"

Cheers and clapping rang out. Hand in hand they stepped down from the ambulance into the waiting crowd of fellow paramedics, troopers, cops, and friends.

Kendall watched as crime scene tape was strung around the limo. A white sheet covered the body of Johnnie Black still in the car. "It's finally over," said Kendall.

"Yes my wife-to-be, it is." He picked her up in his arms. "Shall we go join the bride and groom?" he said sarcastically.

She laughed, kicking her legs in the air. "Put me down you silly man."

Carrying her to a waiting limo, he set her down and opened the door. Inside Andy and CJ waited. The two couples toasted each other with champagne.

"You know next month when we do this for real CJ, I think we'll do a few things differently," said Andy.

"Yeah like skip the dead limo driver," said CJ.

"Definitely less bullets," said Kendall.

"I thought the ceremony was nice," said Mike. He tapped the divider, getting the driver's attention. "Let's skip the once around the park too."

Trooper Connell smiled back. "Whatever you say sir." She hit the gas taking the couples past a group of troopers, cops, and medics making catcalls and whistles.

Birdseed pelted the windows followed by clanking cans and flying streamers.

"To a happy life and new beginning," toasted Andy.

"Cheers!" said Mike, CJ and Kendall. Clinking their glasses together the friends laughed happily.

"You know, we all made a pretty good team," said Kendall.

"Sure did!" said Andy, smiling at his bride to be.

Mike and CJ nodded, smiling from ear to ear.

"I've been thinking that maybe we should offer our services to the general public," said Kendall.

Three sets of eyes focused on her, eyebrows raised.

"We'd work in teams of two—one paramedic and one officer of the law. The best of both worlds."

"And do what exactly?" asked Mike.

"Solve crimes or maybe act as security for the rich and famous. CJ certainly has the connections for that," said Kendall. She looked around expectantly.

"Might not be a bad idea," said CJ, elbowing her husband in the side.

"Wife says I'm in," shrugged Andy.

Mike rolled his eyes. "You guys are crazy."

"I like the name Midnight Riders, Inc.," said Kendall.

"You are nuts!" said Mike.

"Nuts about you sweetie," she said, pinching his cheek.

"Ouch! OK, OK, I'm in," said Mike. Raising his glass he toasted. "To the Midnight Riders!"

Four glasses clanked in unison. "To the Midnight Riders!

Seventy-four

In the crowd, watching the limo drive away, a man frowned. Fighting the urge to pull his forty-five from his coat pocket, he cursed under his breath. The plan had gone horribly wrong.

She wasn't going to get away with this. None of them were. Johnnie and Tommy were dead, leaving him all alone. He ran his fingers through his hair. Putting on his baseball hat, he tapped the front of it with his pointer finger in a mock salute to the receding limo. "Until, until, w...wee maa-eet again!" He turned and walked past his dead lover's body and then disappeared into the crowd.

THE END

Find out what happens next for Kendall Rose and crew.

Book Two of The Kendall Rose Mystery Series

A Simple Case of Revenge

The Horse Avenger serial killer is hell-bent on slaughtering every horse dealer in sight. Kill buyer Kenny Hunter knows the only thing between him and the meat hook is the newly formed Midnight Riders Security, Inc. with Paramedic Kendall Rose and Trooper Mike Garcia at the helm. Seeing dollar signs and fame, Mike agrees to take the case despite objections from several team members, including his fiancé Kendall.

As the team fractures from within, it becomes clear that another killer lurks in the shadows waiting to strike at the very heart of the team. When one of their own is kidnapped by a sexual sadist bent on revenge for the deaths of Johnnie and Tommy Black, will the team reunite to face their greatest foe?

Available on amazon.com

www.ingramcontent.com/pod-product-compliance
Lightning Source LLC
Chambersburg PA
CBHW070811180626
46818CB00001B/216